*Carmel Austin and friends present*

# Courageous
# Voices
# Unlocked

**"Empowered Stories of Moving
from Brokenness to Freedom"**

Carmel's Garden
Shoalhaven NSW
Australia
www.carmelsgarden.com



Published by Carmel Austin Publishing October 17, 2024.

ISBN: 978-0-6458582-5-9 (paperback)
ISBN: 978-0-6458582-4-2 (hardcover)
ISBN: 978-0-6458582-6-6 (eBook)

Library of Congress Control Number: 2024920344


Cover designed by Carmel Austin

Edited by Stephanie Miller (www.butterfly-beginnings.com)

Interior design formatted by Written Words Publishing LLC (writtenwordspublishing.com)

**Carmel's Garden**

**Carmel Austin Publishing**
Unified Voices

I realized I was still carrying a lingering sense of shame from my past. Her chapter beautifully emphasizes the love and forgiveness of Jesus Christ and the new identity we gain as His beloved daughters. In doing so, it became a tool the Lord used to further heal areas within me that I didn't even realize needed healing.

Stephanie also poignantly addresses the reason many women, who as young girls lacked the love of their earthly fathers, often seek to fill that void inappropriately through relationships with men who cannot truly love them. Thankfully, she highlights the Lord's love and mercy, which not only draws us into the arms of our Heavenly Father but also empowers us to forgive our earthly fathers for their shortcomings. I believe this chapter will touch the hearts of many women, offering them hope. Hope that, even if they did not receive the love they needed from their earthly father, and even if this led them into harmful relationships, God can and does rewrite our stories with His forgiveness and love. In Him, we are given a new life filled with His plans and promises for a glorious future. Above all, Stephanie's chapter delivers the transformative message that we are dearly loved by God—a message that truly makes all the difference in the world.

~ **Terry Gassett,** *Certified Licensed Professional Coach*

**Amanda Schaefer's words,** 'I need more than just being free for myself—I want everyone to be free!' perfectly capture the essence of her heart and mission in *Courageous Voices Unlocked.* Touched by the grace of God, Amanda's deepest desire is for others to experience the same glorious freedom she has found. Her genuine love for people shines through in everything she does, and she is always seeking opportunities to share the love of Jesus Christ with those who do not yet know Him. Amanda's writing beautifully reflects her passionate faith, and through her eloquent words, she richly blesses all who read her work.

*~ **Dawn R. Ward**, Author of From Guilt to Grace: Hope and Healing for Christian Moms of Addicted Children, Founder of The Faith to Flourish*

**Teresa Dial's words** struck a deep chord within me, especially when she writes, 'Our souls, like silver, must transfer heat (trials) quickly back to Him to maintain proper function.' This quote resonated profoundly as it encapsulates the essence of the story—a journey from defining beauty through societal lenses to embracing the transformative power of faith. I admired the raw transparency that Teresa brings to the table, addressing everything from harmful acts and workplace struggles to the self-defeating thoughts that ultimately surrender to the name of Jesus.

Her writing is relatable and powerful, capturing the reader's attention from start to finish. For those who value honesty, unsweetened experiences, and the silver lining found by an overcomer in Christ, Teresa's story will undoubtedly resonate deeply.

*~ **Molly Trotter-Gomez**, Co-Founder, Kingdom Alliance, Leadership and Speaker Trainer*

**Dorease Rioux's writing** reflects her admiration for storytellers like CS Lewis, drawing readers into vivid scenes of her encounters with workplace bullies, whom she calls 'the coyotes.' These adversaries, like the bullies we all face, try to overshadow our light for reasons they may not fully understand.

Dorease's heart shines through with compassion, wisdom, and strength in every word. She invites readers into her journey, reminding us: 'I write this from battle scars, not wounds.' Her experiences teach without regret or bitterness, showing how we are often targeted in the areas we are meant to conquer. Her relationship with the Lord is woven throughout, portraying Him as the guide who helps her navigate through challenges and embrace her identity as a 'strong and courageous Braveheart.'

Her chapter encourages readers to exchange fear for love, rejection for acceptance, and shame for honor through Jesus. It's a powerful reminder to embrace our true identity in Christ and rise above life's challenges.

~ *Karen Stally, Co-Founder of The Winning Warrior Network, Author, Speaker, and Certified Life Coach*

**ShonaRobyn's chapter** is a beautiful and powerful message about God's great love for us, especially through times of adversity. She guides us through her own personal journey of self-discovery and weaves her beautiful insights along the way. Her story serves as a poignant reminder of the healing power of nature and how we are all connected as one.

~ *Marie Ramos*

**M. DeAnne Morrell's** chapter, "Ride the Wave of Courage," is an inspiring journey of courage and self-discovery. It showcases the power of stepping outside one's comfort zone and embracing the unknown with grace and determination. DeAnne's storytelling is both heartwarming and relatable, making you feel like you're riding alongside her, experiencing each thrill, challenge, and triumph. From motorcycle rides with her father to mastering the art of riding solo, her chapter beautifully captures the essence of courage.

What stands out is DeAnne's authenticity in sharing her struggles and victories. Her reflections on finding confidence, learning at her own pace, and rekindling her passion after setbacks are relatable and inspiring. Her journey reminds us that self-discovery often involves moments of doubt and fear, but those moments shape us into who we're meant to be. DeAnne calls us all to ride our own waves of courage and embrace our destiny that awaits.

~ *Sue Beck, Worship Leader and Student of Coach MD*

**Nic Henry Jones' story** is a powerful testament to resilience, faith, and transformation. From a young age, Nic felt a call to a higher purpose, navigating personal and professional setbacks that ultimately shaped her into the remarkable person she is today. Her journey, marked by challenges and triumphs, underscores the profound truth that God uses every experience—joyous or painful—to craft a masterpiece out of our lives.

Nic's life now reflects her deep alignment with her faith

and purpose. Through her businesses, books, and leadership roles, she is committed to helping others discover their identity in God. Her story serves as a poignant reminder that no matter how difficult the journey, hope and potential abound when we align with our true identity in God.

~ *Maree Cutler Naroba,* *Founder, The Deborah Business Education Hub & Deborah Conference, Business Strategist, Author*

**Cynthia Kelly's** chapter, *Divine Dialogue,* is a profound exploration of the power of words and faith. Cynthia seamlessly intertwines personal experiences with spiritual insights, crafting a narrative that is both inspiring and transformative. This work offers more than just a reflection on the impact of words; it is a powerful testament to the significance of aligning our thoughts and speech with God's truth. Truly a remarkable read!

~ *Andrew Sutherland*

**Catherine's story** is a testament to her remarkable journey of self-reflection and understanding of life's experiences, both challenging and positive, that have shaped her. Her writing beautifully encapsulates how an inner voice finds strength through kindness to others, the joys found in music, and, most importantly, an unwavering love, trust, and faith in God.

God bless your journey of self-care, Catherine.

~ *Cei Harris*

# TABLE OF CONTENTS

# PREFACE

Welcome to *Courageous Voices Unlocked*, where you will journey alongside a unique group of courageous women who have faced life's most challenging trials with unwavering determination. This book is more than a collection of stories; it's a powerful testament to the human spirit's ability to confront fears, embrace vulnerabilities, and bravely step into the unknown.

As co-authors, we've come together to shine a light on the many paths of courage that reside within us all. Each chapter serves as a window into our souls, offering insights into resilience, faith, and the will to rise above life's daunting challenges.

From the depths of infertility to unearthing hidden dreams, from reclaiming heritage to overcoming destructive habits, from healing trauma to finding God's grace and love, these narratives weave a rich tapestry of human experience. Each story is a thread in this fabric, contributing to a mosaic of emotions, hard-earned wisdom, and enduring hope. Though our stories are diverse, we are united by a common thread—the relentless pursuit of purpose and the courage to turn pain into the power of our testimony.

*Courageous Voices Unlocked* is more than just a book; it is a sanctuary for those who dare to dream, refuse to be defined by their circumstances, and seek to unleash their authentic voices. As the visionary and lead author, I find this project deeply personal, and every story shared holds a piece of my heart.

Throughout these pages, you may see reflections of your own struggles and triumphs. You might find solace in knowing you are not alone and inspiration in how others have navigated their paths from brokenness to Freedom. This anthology is a reminder that, no matter how broken we may feel, within each of us lies the seed of redemption, nurtured by the courage to speak our truths so others may walk in freedom and courage.

I hope these courageous voices resonate with you on your own journey. As we reflect on the impact of The Artist Haven, the first book that brought together many of these powerful stories, it's inspiring to see some of the same authors return for this sequel. Alongside their voices, we also welcome new storytellers who bring fresh perspectives. The friendships and connections forged through our shared experiences continue to grow, extending beyond the pages and enriching our lives.

As you explore *Courageous Voices Unlocked*, may you find the strength to embrace your own journey with renewed energy and resolve. Let these stories accompany you on your path, recognising that our shared experiences have the power to awaken the courage within each of us. May you be inspired to step into your greater destiny as you embrace the truths and bravery these pages reveal.

With heartfelt gratitude,

*Coach Carmel Austin and the Co-Authors of Courageous Voices Unlocked*

# DEDICATION

To my Dad, Ignazio Spaccavento 'Tassy Spacc,' my Hero:

Even though you faced your own challenges in life, you always showed me love and acceptance through your discipline, sense of humor, and skills in dancing, playing tola, and snooker. Even when it was hard for me to understand as a little girl, you were there for me. Now, as a mature woman who loves life and embraces my uniqueness, I am deeply grateful for your unwavering love and support. Though you are now in heaven with our family, I miss you with everything that is within me every day and will always carry you and Mum in my heart, actions, and thoughts. Thank you for everything, Daddy.

Your loving daughter, Carmel xx

# ECHOES OF HOPE
## CONFRONTING THE UNEXPECTED

## Carmel Austin

Wholeness Coach, Artisan, Podcaster,
Publisher & Digital Growth Mentor

**Shoalhaven NSW, Australia**

*"Beyond grief of loss is a road less travelled,
that takes you into your greater destiny."*
~ Carmel Austin

**Navigating the Depths: My Journey Through Infertility and Beyond**

In the quiet corridors of my heart, a story has been unfolding for decades. It's a tale of loss, grief, and the unyielding hope that continues to burn within me.

I've poured my thoughts, prayers, and emotions into journals piling up in a cupboard, each line etched with the intention to light a path for women navigating infertility and loss. It's been an odyssey of both highs and lows, filled with hospital visits, surgeries, and the profound emotional struggles that accompany my journey into wholeness.

Life, as I've come to understand, is a treasure trove of experiences waiting to be uncovered. I invite you to join me on a journey of exploration—a journey that led me to discover the tapestry of my heritage and the deep-seated dreams that define my heart.

As a woman marred by the shame of infertility and loss, I

often convinced myself that I was alone in my grief, creating an isolating parallel world that trapped me. But I stand here today to proclaim that I am not alone. I have travelled those same rocky roads, and I understand the pain, the confusion, and the yearning for a community that comprehends the language of grief, a community that would be able to help me move toward the endless opportunities of freedom and grace.

The labyrinth of grief is never traversed with ease, especially when faced with the stark reality that the arms I long to cradle my children in will remain empty on this earth. It's a pain that pierces the heart's deepest recesses, a constant, slow leak of hopes and dreams lost. I have ascended to the mountaintops of triumph and plunged into the valleys of despair, living on an emotional roller coaster. Yet, through it all, I've discovered that I can find a way forward, embracing the journey with courage and finding the grace that awaits on the other side.

Amidst these storms of doubt and fear, a heavenly voice bid me to take a leap of faith. It was an eleventh-hour encounter with destiny, as God's presence materialized when I stood at the crossroads of disappointment and desperation. Just when I believed that the dreams nestled in my heart were fading, an Angelic whisper rekindled the flame within me. It was the miraculous birth of a new chapter, a testament that even amidst the darkest moments, heaven had plans for me.

I've toiled with diligence, hands on the plow, working toward my aspirations and life goals. I've learned to trust the 90-degree turns that God presents, even when disappointment looms large. This trust has led me to a revelation: realising the longing for my own biological children doesn't diminish my identity as a woman. Instead, it propels me to embrace my other God-given talents, empowering me to transmute my story into a source of encouragement for others.

My journey to becoming a wholeness coach has taken its own path. Investing in myself to follow my dreams has unfolded in unexpected ways, guiding me through various roles as an entrepreneur, artist, coach, and mentor. When I was young, I always felt like I was different, standing out from the crowd and speaking my mind, expressing my mother's heart beyond my capacity, and stretching my tent pegs wider than I ever imagined.

I spent a lot of time creating pictures and coming up with ideas outside the box, dreaming of writing and role-playing as a child, standing on stages, and leading others on a unique journey of adventure and experiences. I was always dreaming that life was mine to create and become whoever I wanted. At times, I thought that role play and dreaming was a coping mechanism to help me through very difficult days of not fitting into the world and trying to live up to people's false expectations.

Reflecting on my childhood, I realise life was not always pleasant, despite having a loving home with parents who provided for us. I had friends, went to school, and had my whole life ahead of me. But things took a turn when I was held back in fifth grade due to a lack of understanding that I am unique. My life struggles living with dyslexia and Irlen syndrome made me feel different. I had to repeat 5th class because the teacher misunderstood my learning ability and the transition to a new group of classmates brought its own set of challenges.

Entering a new classroom, I faced immense adversity with my studies and the nun who was both my teacher and the principal for three years. Having to stay in the same room with the class set up as a co-learning room with 5th and 6th-grade girls, I found myself among girls who didn't understand me and had their own emotional issues to deal with. I became the target of bad behaviour that caused me to be oppressed, enduring terrible treatment that left me feeling overwhelmed and lost. My mum did her best to support me, but the damage was done, and I struggled to cope with the emotional and physical toll it took on me.

It took a long time for me to discover my true healthy identity. I was well into my fifties when I began to understand more about myself and the challenges I faced. I started to understand my struggles were not just academic but rooted in traumatic experiences, including a near-drowning incident at a young age. These revelations have helped me piece together the puzzle of my lost identity and understand why I felt different from others.

One of the most profound lessons I learned on my journey was the importance of forgiveness. Despite the pain and hurt I experienced, discovering the power of forgiveness and accepting myself as a unique creation, beautifully made as a woman in God's image, allowed me to forgive myself, my family, and my peers who I felt had judged and hurt me.

I knew holding onto bitterness would only weigh me down. I had to forgive myself for thinking I did not fit in and forgive those who I felt had wronged me. Through forgiveness, I found freedom and the ability to move forward with my life. This newfound forgiveness enabled me to embark on a journey of self-love and discovery, deepening my relationship with my Heavenly Father who loves me unconditionally.

As I continued to heal, I embraced purpose and community. I realised my story was meant to be shared. I embarked on a journey of self-expression through writing and creating art which brings healing and balance to my soul, connecting with other like-minded creatives who share similar experiences. Building a community of support and inclusivity has become my mission, I love to encourage others to embrace their uniqueness and walk out their divine purpose.

Today, I am grateful for the opportunity to empower other creatives on their own journeys of healing and self-discovery. Through coaching and collaboration, I love to help people, especially women, break free from the chains of bitterness and step into their true potential. My hope is that by sharing my story and offering support, I can inspire others to embrace forgiveness, find their voice, and live a life of fulfillment and purpose.

In the past, it seemed like I was always speaking up for the lost and lonely, the broken-hearted and the misfits. I believe I was searching to be accepted and express my creative self in all its uniqueness. Today as the author I am now sharing my narrative with the world. Through each twist and turn, I've gleaned wisdom, drawing strength from my multicultural upbringing and the challenges it posed. Our home was filled with multiple languages spoken and with my dyslexia, I struggled with who I was, why I was on this earth, and where I fitted in. The hurdles I faced have shaped my determination and drive, pushing me to excel in areas where my talents naturally bloomed.

Attending art classes and learning how to sew as a young girl brought me much freedom to express my creativity and shine through my natural talents. I seemed to always be struggling to keep up with my peers when it came to academic skills and those who seemed to have their lives sorted. I was clouded by rose-coloured glasses.

Never in my wildest imagination did I think that when I entered my early 40s I would start wearing blue-tinted glasses to help my brain function better and cope with everyday tasks that life brings my way and be diagnosed with Irlen syndrome.

*"Life's challenges and winding paths have shaped me into the strong, confident, compassionate woman I am today. I embrace my purpose with creativity and a deep love for life."*

## Destiny Unearthed: Embracing Hidden Dreams and Heritage

As we continue to journey through the corridors of my life, I want to unveil a phase that has been instrumental in shaping my creative expression and becoming the person I am today. This phase marked a time of exploration, a period where I travelled the ancient roads of destiny and discovered more of my family heritage, unearthing the hidden dreams that were tucked away in the recesses of my heart.

In 2010, walking the pebble-stone roads of Israel, I traced my ancestors' footsteps to the Holy Land and the shores of Lebanon. I sought to understand the threads that wove the fabric of my identity as a Christian, daughter and wife, born into a traditional Catholic family. I wanted to explore more of my Lebanese roots, uncovering stories of resilience, courage, and unwavering faith. This voyage into the past provided a mirror into the essence of who I am today, infusing my journey with a profound sense of purpose.

But this journey wasn't just about tracing footsteps; it was about stepping into my footprints of destiny. It was a call to embrace my dreams that have long whispered in the chambers of my heart. As I ventured deeper, I discovered hidden aspirations, and passions that had been waiting for their moment in the spotlight.

The path of exploring one's heritage and destiny is not always linear. It's a tapestry woven with threads of both certainty and uncertainty, familiarity and novelty. It's about honoring where you come from while embracing the journey that lies ahead. Through this process, I found more of my voice as a creative artisan and entrepreneur—a voice that resonates with the wisdom of generations gone by.

What dreams lie dormant within you?

What heritage shapes the core of your being?

I invite you to embrace this moment, for within it lies the opportunity to uncover hidden treasures and paint the canvas of your destiny.

Amidst my travels, a dream from my younger days resurfaced, reminding me of my desire to explore the world and leave an impact. This dream inspired me to recall my aspiration as a young woman who wanted to travel the world as a singer and build a loving family, dreams intertwined as messy threads of my life, the life source that keeps the blood pumping to my heart. This road hasn't been easy—I met my husband at the tender age of sixteen, we have overcome countless disappointments together, including grappling with our shared yearning for parenthood. Our journey of loss and grief has been instrumental in shaping the person I am today.

Life's journey and the path we have walked together have led us through a garden of diverse experiences, from establishing my business, "Carmel's Garden," to seeking fulfillment through artistic expression. The pinnacle of this voyage arrived when I stood at the precipice of my calling as a writer. Despite my dyslexia and early childhood struggles of not being able to spell or read, and facing tantrums and pain—I became an overcomer.

Reflecting on how far I've come to learn, grow, and nurture others, I feel privileged and blessed to help people bring their dreams to life, share their stories, and find their voices.

It isn't without challenges. The recent sudden loss of my father tore through my world, leaving me grappling with grief. Yet, even in the midst of pain, I found solace in my commitment to his well-being and the fulfillment of promises made to my mother. The words well done, good, and faithful daughter rings true in my heart. This experience deepened my resolve to help others find their own significance and purpose.

This road has shown me that life isn't about succumbing to fears or retreating from dreams. Instead, it's about embracing challenges, expressing yourself authentically, and nurturing the seeds of potential that lie within you. My story speaks to those who have endured similar trials, encouraging them to stand tall, reclaim their voices, and chase after their dreams.

Stepping into this new chapter of my life, I have found myself guiding other women on their journeys as a wholeness coach and mentor. I now offer my hand to you, dear reader. If you are looking for the road less travelled and would like guidance on this road? Let's embark on a journey together, crafting narratives that uplift, inspire, and heal.

*"For amid our struggles, triumphs, and dreams,
we are united by the thread of our shared humanity."*

## Unleashing Dreams: Transforming Fear into Faith

In the grandstand of life, each of us carries dreams within our hearts—dreams that sparkle with hope, resonate with purpose, and beckon us to reach beyond our limitations. Yet, how often do these dreams remain locked within, silenced by the voices of doubt and fear? I'm here to tell you that those dreams are worth chasing, worth fighting for, and worth believing in.

Stepping away from my doubts to become a wholeness coach, embracing my creativity, and sharing my story of loss has been a transformative journey. My dreams of motherhood were shattered, but in 2021, I took the bold step of building my new website and began opening up about my personal experiences. From there, I expanded my story through my books and podcast show *The Thriving Woman*. Now, I've grown into the role of guiding other creatives, helping them publish their stories as I illustrate books and magazines, and encourage my clients and co-authors to build lives filled with purpose and value.

*'I am a pint-size girl with a big heart of
dreams and visions being born and fulfilled.'*

Instead of allowing fear of the unknown to stop me from moving forward and pursuing my God-given dreams to become the person I am today. I embarked upon a journey of discovery to share my story and see the visions and dreams in my heart unearthed even though I moved forward with uncertainty gnawing at the corners of my mind.

Living with multiple health issues and having to overcome my fears and turn them into abilities has been difficult at times. I struggled at school with basic skills like writing, grammar homework, and fitting into what was the status quo. When you suffer from the fear of not fitting in, you tend to hide a lot of truths and put on a brave face to the world. The path I envisioned was at times a daunting one—filled with aspirations of speaking at conferences, launching coaching programs, and leaving an indelible mark on the world. Yet, the shadows of doubt whispered, "Who are you to dream so big? What if you fail?"

But friends, we are humans who navigate tumultuous waters at times. We may stumble upon the life-changing truth that Scripture holds. A divine invitation resounds: *"Ask of me, and I will make the nations your inheritance, the ends of the earth your possession"* (Psalm 2:8 NIV). It's as if the Creator Himself urges us to cast aside our hesitations and approach our dreams with boldness.

Again. I encourage you to take the time to search out the ancient pages of the Holy Book where truths are revealed that can inspire and lift you out of despair giving you courage and hope.

> *"So do not throw away your confidence; it will be richly rewarded. You need to persevere so that when you have done the will of God, you will receive what he has promised"*
> (Hebrews 10:35-36 NIV).

These words echoed within me, they remind me that the journey may be riddled with challenges, but the destination—ah, the destination is worth the climb.

I invite you to stand at the crossroads of fear and move into faith, choose this day the path less travelled. It's a path that beckons you to silence the disheartening voices of the past and replace them with affirmations of unwavering faith.

> *"Your dreams are not mere fantasies, but divine callings etched into your soul. They are gifts from the Creator, inviting you to take the time to unwrap, look inside, and discover the treasures of life."*

As we venture forth, let's remember the wisdom of the ancient scriptures which encourages us to:

*"Not neglect your gift, which was given you through prophecy when the body of elders laid their hands on you. Be diligent in these matters; give yourself wholly to them, so that everyone may see your progress"* (1 Timothy 4:14-15 NIV).

In the pages of this book that follow, let's unearth the power of dreams. Let's learn how to replace hesitation with audacity, fear with faith, and doubt with determination.

Together, we have journeyed and unlocked the doors to a reality where dreams flourish, with my co-authors and clients as they grow as influencers expanding their capacity to reach for the stars and shine as beacons of light to the next generation.

*"This is my new reality where lives radiate with purpose, inspiring others to shed their fears and march resolutely toward their destinies."*

## Full Circle: From Silence to Strength

Reflecting on the final chapter of my international co-author book, "The Artist Haven," my friend LaTrina Bray bravely shares her infertility journey. This once-silent struggle of loss is now voiced. As women we used to feel alone, facing the emptiness where a child's laughter should be, enduring hospital visits, procedures, and profound emotional and physical pain.

But now, we're no longer alone. We've opened our hearts to friends like you about our journey, and it's made all the difference. Walking together, hand in hand, we've lightened the tough road. We support each other, lifting one another with prayers and encouragement, creating courageous voices.

So, dear friend, I encourage you to join us on this journey. Let's let our dreams reshape our reality, leaving behind doubts and embracing the faith that guides our every step.

As you continue to turn the pages of this book, I invite you to step into the intricate tapestry of my life and my co-authors'. Our stories are woven with threads of loss, grief, and the undying flame of hope. It's a journey that spans decades, marked by divorce, loss, dreams dashed, hospital visits, surgeries, and the unrelenting emotional roller coaster of infertility and lost lives. Yet, amidst these trials, we found faith and a new life.

We are now living from a place of victory, not shame. We encourage you to Imagine, for a moment, a road less travelled—a path that leads to the greatest accomplishments that lie beyond the boundaries of our human limitations. It's a journey where our dreams take on a life of their own, where our aspirations soar with the wings of possibility. This journey beckons each author with their courageous voice to share their stories, daring to push you beyond your comfort zone.

> *"Let's embrace the uncharted, moving beyond*
> *fears and into great accomplishments."*

## Dear Fellow Traveller,

As we embark on this journey together, I urge you to leave behind the shadows of the past, the haunting fears that have kept you confined. Now is the time to adopt a new outlook, one that leads us toward the uncharted landscapes of our dreams. In this space, I invite you to cast off the weight of regret and disappointment, stepping beyond the corridors they've built. Here, we find a realm of freedom and grace, where we transform pain into growth and embrace freedom as both shield and guide.

Encouraging you to rise above the echoes of past traumas, knowing it's no easy feat, yet a journey worth undertaking. Just as a caterpillar must leave behind its cocoon to emerge as a butterfly, we too must release the layers that no longer serve us. This is a process of transformation, a journey from the confinements of our past into the radiance of our potential.

The paths of regret and disappointment may be long and winding, but they need not define our course. Instead, they serve as steppingstones, reminders of our resilience and our capacity to overcome.

I ask you to take the time to read this book and allow yourself to launch into the realms of greatness, allowing the accomplishments of my authors to transcend the limitations of your mind.

Dreams are not limited to what we can easily imagine. They're vast, imaginative, and beyond what we might initially think possible they are capable of propelling us beyond the boundaries we've imposed. As we step into the unknown, let us remember that even the greatest accomplishments began as dreams. It's the audacious dreamers who challenge the status quo and pave the way for new horizons.

In closing I again highlight the road less travelled and reflect that it is not always well-marked; it requires courage, determination, and an unwavering belief in our potential. But in the uncharted, we find the fertile ground for growth, the canvas for our grandest accomplishments. Our journey may not be easy, but it is the very challenges we face that mold us into the architects of our destinies.

So, let's journey onward, leaving behind the weight of what once was. Let's dream big, embracing the vast expanse of our potential. The road less travelled calls us, and its promise is vast—a promise of accomplishments that transcend the limitations of our past, propelling us toward a future where we stand triumphant.

With courage as our compass, let's step beyond our comfort zones and forge ahead. This is a journey of a lifetime, a journey into the realm of the extraordinary.

Yours in audacious dreaming,

*Carmel Austin*

Wholeness Life Coach, #1 International Bestselling Author, Publisher, Podcaster, Visionary, and Writing Mentor

The poem on the next page, "The Road Less Travelled," is dedicated to my seven angels—my precious babies who were carried within me but never had the chance to be held in my arms. They shine brightly in Heaven, always close to me, reminding me of their love and presence. Forever alive in my heart, dreams, and hopes, they guide me, surrounding me with their light and love.

## The Road Less Travelled

"Amid shattered dreams, lie treasures yet unseen,
In every heart, dreams dwell, fading to regrets, unseen,
Eyes closed tight 'gainst pain and despair,
Finding solace in love's embrace, beyond compare.

On the brink of awakening in eternity's glow,
Where dreams thrive eternal, love's endless flow,
Do not despair, dear heart, for dreams are alive,
In heaven's embrace, where new paths arrive.

Grief, a fleeting season, gives way to hope's light,
A prayer of belief, leading onward to life's flight,
Step by step through cosmos unknown,
Where dreams and hopes merge, in love's sweet tone."

# ABOUT THE AUTHOR

Carmel Austin is a #1 International bestselling author, speaker, and wholeness life coach. She founded Carmel's Garden, a ministry empowering women and families to integrate creativity with spiritual growth. In her books, *Just Say No, Dear Superwoman,* and *The Artist Haven,* Carmel shares her personal journey as a writer and coach, offering insights into balancing creativity and business ownership. Carmel dedicates significant time to illustrating and designing covers for her books and crafting articles for *Mystery of Eden* magazine through Carmel Austin Publishing.

As the host of *The Thriving Woman* podcast, available on Spotify and YouTube, Carmel interviews creatives and coaches, sharing wisdom on living authentically and achieving creative growth. Beyond writing and coaching, Carmel is a sought-after speaker, leading workshops and mentoring sessions focused on transforming lives through creativity.

When not immersed in her coaching practice, Carmel enjoys family time, camping, and creating heirloom quilts. Her passion lies in helping creatives thrive by rewriting their inner stories and embracing their authentic selves.

On Amazon, you can find Carmel's books.

Each collaborative-book project has achieved #1 International Bestseller status:

*The Artist Haven*
*Dear Superwoman*
*Just Say No*

*Just Say No* can be purchased from Carmel's website at www.carmelsgarden.com/shop-carmelsgarden-shop-just-say-no-book

**Find Me:**

Facebook:
www.facebook.com/carmelsgarden
www.facebook.com/carmel.austin1

Instagram:
www.instagram.com/carmelsgardenwholenesscoach

YouTube: www.youtube.com/@carmelsgarden

LinkedIn: www.linkedin.com/in/carmelsgarden

Website: www.carmelsgarden.com

Email: carmelsgardenpublish@gmail.com

Gift for you: www.carmelsgarden.com/free-gift-carmels-garden-become-an-author

# COURAGEOUS VOICES UNLOCKED

*Reflecting on my journey to self-worth, I'm reminded of the victory and freedom that came with finding the courage to speak up, all thanks to God's incredible work in my life. Shame comes in all different shapes and sizes and my next beautiful co-author and friend, **Stephanie** will share her story of God's grace and redemption through "tacos, shoes, and the good news."*

# Dedication

To my daughters, Abigail and Tabitha, may you always know that you are deeply loved, not for what you do, but for who you are.

To the younger generations of women searching for love, worth, and meaning in all the wrong places—there is only ONE answer to the emptiness you feel, and His name is Jesus.

To everyone who feels like their story is "too much," "too shocking," or "too extreme"—your story matters because you matter.

To those who dare to boldly and courageously share your story for His glory—God sees you, and He loves you.

"Your story may very well be the key that unlocked healing in another person."

And I pray that my story does just that.

Stephanie Miller

# Tacos, Shoes and the Good News
## A Redemption Story

## Stephanie Miller

Writing and Spiritual Growth Coach

**Tennessee, USA**

*"Above all, love each other deeply, because love covers over a multitude of sins"* (1 Peter 4:8 NIV).

## Searching for Love

My life was a series of toxic relationships, destructive decisions and risky hook-ups from my late teens to my early 20s. I took the "you have to kiss a lot of frogs to find your prince" saying a little too seriously.

I didn't know it then, but I was waiting for my prince charming, my knight-in-shining armor to come rescue me. And he did—but not in the way I imagined.

Growing up in an alcoholic household was chaotic at best, and traumatic at worst. I suppose there was love, but it wasn't love for me. It was love for the bottle, love for the high and try as I might—I could never capture my daddy's attention quite like his six pack of Zima could.

Psychologists call this "love-starved." I was love-starved and hungry for love and looking for it in all the wrong places. In my desperation to feel wanted and desired I sacrificed my dignity and my pride.

It's like when you really want tacos from your favorite Mexican restaurant but opt for the quick fix of *Taco Bell*, only to end up feeling crappy the next day. It never quite satisfies.

There is a reason they call it the walk of shame.

Yet, for as shameful and disgusted I felt as the walk of shame became a routine for me—there was something inside of me, a deeper need I was desperate to fill that spurred me on to try to search out the one thing I longed for…love.

Not counterfeit love, but real love. I didn't know it at the time, but that's really what I wanted. I went around trying to fill the God-shaped hole in my heart with whatever I thought would be the answer to all my problems at the time. Never mind the fact that most of my "problems" were brought on by false beliefs about myself and the decisions I made in the attempts to find happiness.

As the saying goes, I went looking for love in all the wrong places. And even when I gave my life to Jesus while dating a Christian guy in college—it wasn't enough. His innocence intrigued me, but I saw his conservative shell as a challenge for me to get through.

My need to feel desired overshadowed everything else. As much as I hate to admit it, it was all a game to me. It wasn't enough that I had a boyfriend, I wanted other guys to pay attention and notice me as well. I could play the "sweet girlfriend" role quite well.

But I found myself trying to live up to his standard and having a difficult time. Then, after choosing to cheat on him with my ex-boyfriend (ironically, doing the very thing *with* him that I did *to* him) it all came crashing down—again.

So, I retreated to the life I knew, parties and promiscuity.

You know that old pair of shoes you keep in your closet that you just can't bring yourself to get rid of? The ones that are worn out, full of holes and no longer offer any support for your feet. They really don't do anything for you, but they are just so comfortable that you find yourself wearing them repeatedly out of habit. That's how my life of sin felt for me, completely useless—but familiar.

I saw myself in a cycle that I couldn't get out of. Part of me enjoyed the lust, the passion, the risk and the excitement. The other part of me, however, was desperate to get out of the habit of taking things too far. And when heavy drinking was involved, as it almost always was, the objectified attention I craved was never in short supply.

It was a dead-end road. I was chasing happiness, instant gratification, and pleasure. But I was empty and hollow—just existing.

## Painful Memories

In some ways, I may have been just living out what psychologists call a self-fulfilling prophecy. Which is a fancy way of saying when you believe something to be true you make choices and decisions that support that belief.

I have a memory of when I was in high school, and I was dressed up for some occasion. I asked my dad how I looked. I'm sure I wanted him to say beautiful or pretty, but instead he chose to call me a derogatory name.

Looking back, this could have been his way of trying to say he cared, and I shouldn't go out of the house dressed that way, but I didn't see it at the time. Addiction makes people do and say horrible things, and even the fondness a dad inherently has for his daughter can be tainted through substance abuse.

I'm not saying that he is responsible for the choices I made, but I am saying believing my dad saw me this way and thinking these things about myself—I thought I could never be anyone different.

Another example of this, which isn't as extreme, has to do with conversations I had with my mom as a young teenager. She shared with me her own struggles with her self-esteem and self-confidence and told me that as a teenager herself she built a reputation of being a "tease."

In my adolescent mind, I decided that if she could get attention from boys and not do things, then I could get more attention from boys by…well, you know where I'm going with this.

Carrying this mindset into my college years, I started to spin out of control.

I believed the lie that I had to act a certain way and be a certain way to attract attention from men. The decisions I made during this time in my life were selfish, toxic and dangerous. I thought the only way for someone to value and appreciate me was to lead with my promiscuity.

And I succeeded. I had the attention I wanted from men. I was quite desired. But I found myself developing feelings for hook-ups that were never reciprocated, so the downward spiral continued.

Sometimes I was interested only in getting them interested in me, and other times I wanted a real relationship, but that thought never crossed their minds.

Then I met my husband-to-be, Nick.

## A New Beginning

I always had a thing for clean-cut, wholesome guys. I was drawn to their innocence because I saw them as a challenge, and even though I called them naïve, part of me wished I could be like them.

Clean.

Pure.

Innocent.

I thought that I had gone too far down the "bad girl trail" that I could not turn back. I figured that I had set my reputation in stone, and I could never be the "good girl" that someone would want to marry.

It was right after I had a fling with a guy who dropped me faster than a hot potato did the man who would eventually become my husband enter my life.

And, let me tell you, it wasn't love at first sight. But God used the beginning of our relationship to show me what real love is. When he showed up for me in a way I didn't think any man would or could—my opinion of him changed in the blink of an eye.

I was working as a swim coach at the time and on my way to a swim meet when I ran into car issues. I had just started dating Nick, it was a new relationship, and I was still testing the waters because unlike all my other relationships—I didn't want to rip his clothes off the moment I saw him. So, yeah, this way of experiencing mutual attraction and affection was new to me.

I didn't know who else to call when my car broke down, so I called him. Bracing myself for the pushback of, "I'm busy", "I can't" or "Can you ask someone else", you can imagine my surprise when without hesitating, he said he'd be right there. No questions asked.

Oh, did I mention it was pouring down rain and it was at least a 50 min drive from where he lived to where my car broke down? But he showed up, ready to help—no questions asked.

This was the first time a man I dated ever showed up for me when it didn't benefit him in some way.

In fact, he showed up when it cost him something. His time, his gas, and his Saturday afternoon.

His commitment, dependability, care and concern left me speechless, but I saw him in a whole new way after that incident.

We had not thrown out the word "love" yet, but that's exactly what he was doing. He was showing me love. What it looks like to love another person, the way that we are called to love others.

While I didn't fall in love with Jesus until many years later—I did fall in love with my boyfriend at the time.

This type of love he was showing me was foreign to me, I didn't understand it, and I didn't understand why I was so drawn to him, but I was—in a new way I had never experienced before.

As our relationship progressed, I felt the pressure to tell him about my past. I was sure I would lose him once I told him who I was before I met him.

I didn't.

While I know he didn't fully understand who I was before, he accepted I had a past. But he also told me that he didn't judge me for it, he only saw me for who I was with him at that time, and even more for the future he saw us having together.

*The future.* He saw a future with me. I wasn't too much for him. And even better, he chose me.

Knowing that he chose me as his wife stirred a little hope in me that perhaps I was worth something after all.

*I must be worth something to him, right?*

It's the question I asked myself over and over again as I struggled to feel good enough, and if I'm being honest still struggle with today.

In my quest to find these answers and feel fulfilled, I turned to Jesus.

Not because a boy I liked was a "Jesus freak."

Not because I thought it was what I was "supposed to do."

But because my heart was desperate for love, the type of love that only He could fill.

When Jesus pulled me out of the pit, He set me free.

*"He lifted me out of the slimy pit, out of the mud and mire; he set my feet on a rock and gave me a firm place to stand"* (Psalm 40:2 NIV).

Looking back to who I was before Christ, can, if I'm not careful, evoke shame and embarrassment in me.

I can get in my head about the person I used to be, and what I was about for so long.

The nicknames I had and the reputation I set for myself because, *hey at least with a reputation you are noticed.*

I had a name, I had a label, and I had an identity.

But when Jesus entered the picture, He changed my story.

There is a post on social media about how only God can change our past and our name and it references Rahab, who she was known as in the Old Testament compared to the New Testament.

Joshua 2: *"Rahab, the prostitute"*

Matthew 1: "Rahab, the grandmother of the Messiah, Jesus."

**God changes labels and rewrites stories.**
*What label is God changing for you?*
What strikes me most about this is that her past did not exempt God from using her. First with the spies and second as who she became (the mother to Boaz and grandmother to Jesus). She was no longer known for what (or who) she did, but who she was.

Shame might have been part of her past, but it wasn't part of her future.

The Lord redeemed her past and gave her a future…even more than that…chose her to be part of the lineage in which Jesus came from.

*"Therefore, there is now no condemnation for those who are in Christ Jesus"* (Romans 8:1 NIV).

Your past does not disqualify you from being used to advance the kingdom of God. I don't care who you were, what you did, how you behaved then… All that matters is who you are in Christ—now.

Chosen

Precious

Fearfully and wonderfully made

Beloved.

Everything we do and we are created to be comes first from who we are in Christ.

You can't move from brokenness to freedom without Jesus. And you can't experience the type of love we were created to receive and to give without first experiencing the love of Christ.

And for me, the love of Christ is barely comprehendible. I still have to work to accept that God is our Heavenly Father. I didn't get a good picture of what a father's love looks like from my earthly father, so I have learned how to let God love me so I could learn to love myself and love others.

There has been a lot of unlearning and unraveling to dismantle my idea of what it means to be a perfect daughter.

I tried to be the daughter my dad was proud of, and once I received the approval from him that I hungered for most of my life, surprisingly (or not surprising at all), it still didn't satisfy.

I wanted my dad's approval to be the healing balm over all my wounds, but it wasn't. The void still existed.

Then I realized I was, in fact, looking for love in all the wrong places.

*"We love because he first loved us"* (1 John 4:19 NIV).

It turns out, loving myself and loving others the way God intends only comes from allowing God to love me.

In opening my eyes to Jesus, really surrendering every single part of myself, including who I used to be, He transformed me on the outside as well as the inside.

Outwardly, drinking and partying no longer sounded fun to me. Inappropriate jokes and sexual behavior didn't seem like a good idea anymore.

Even cussing became offensive to me, I would wince when curse words were thrown around, never mind the fact that I used to throw them around like confetti.

Inwardly, I started to feel loveable and accepted. God healed my binge-eating disorder and several others my hurts from my childhood.

The gap of who I thought I needed to be and who I am started to close. I truly became a new person, a new creation.

*"Therefore, if anyone is in Christ, the new creation has come: The old has gone, the new is here!"* (2 Corinthians 5:17 NIV).

All good, right?

Well, despite giving my life to Jesus, and recommitting to Him, there was one area, even up to as recently as last year that I stubbornly held onto. Call it fear, call it pride, call it embarrassment, it was the final area I surrendered to Him last fall, and I haven't looked back.

Below is what the pastor read aloud the day I took my faith public through water baptism. In many ways, this was an expression and declaration of following Jesus, and what allowing Him to love me looked like.

*I've always made 1000 excuses for not being baptized. I've let what others think of me hold me back from taking this next step, I'm a Christian author, life coach, and speaker and yet I've never gone public with my faith. Until now. God has been working on my heart ever since we started attending this church in July 2021. I think the first service we ever attended had several baptisms. Ever since then, when I witness someone get baptized and boldly proclaim their faith in Jesus, I feel an overwhelming sense of joy, but if I'm honest, I get a little more upset with myself as well.*

*"If they can go up there and get baptized, why can't I? Why am I so afraid to take this next step that God has asked me to take?" What tipped me over the edge was when Pastor Steven said that he didn't get baptized until seminary. If there ever was a church body that would celebrate with me for making this declaration and not judge me, I feel like it's this one. My hope is that my honesty and my willingness to put my pride aside to take the plunge (pun intended) will inspire others to do the same. In life we can have comfort and growth, but not both at the same time. Today I'm choosing growth. My prayer is that this one small step of faith and obedience continues to make a kingdom impact for years to come. May my YES to God inspire your YES as well.*

There is only one thing I really remember in that moment. After going under in the baptismal and coming out I felt:

Chosen
Precious
Fearfully and wonderfully made
Beloved.

I explained it to my friend this way. My life after Jesus entered the picture I felt wanted in the way of an engagement. You know, the step before the big commitment.

And when I emerged from the water and I was baptized, I felt—betrothed.

Claimed. His bride.

And not his as in my husband's (although, yes that is true). But His as in God's. I am God's precious child. And so are you.

So, no, my big rescue moment didn't come from a man saving me from my promiscuous ways, instead it came from God's saving grace.

And that is enough for me.

## The Best Hero Ever

I wrote a poem about how my daddy was my hero as a young girl, or at least I wanted him to be. I can't find that poem today to share, but I do remember the last line of the poem:

"My hero, my daddy, come back to me,
I love you, but do you love me?"

Now as an adult, I see that my daddy couldn't be my hero—he was never meant to play that part. I had mistakenly given him shoes to wear that only our Heavenly Father can fill.

My oldest daughter said it best right before she was baptized, just 2 weeks after me… (don't you just love how God uses our YES to Him in such a beautiful and unexpected way?)

"God is the best hero ever."

And I must say, I agree.

To my 20-something-year-old self, you didn't realize it at the time, but you'll soon discover that His love covers a multitude of sins. All your past mistakes and painful choices will be redeemed for your good and His glory. If I were to rewrite that last line of my poem today, here is what I would say:

My Hero, my Heavenly Father,
Thank you for never leaving or forsaking me.
I love you, and I know as your
Precious, chosen, cherished and beloved daughter
You love me—unconditionally.

~ What are some "quick fixes" you've turned to in your life to fill an emptiness or need? How did those choices ultimately impact you?

~ Reflect on a time when you sought love or validation in the wrong places. How did those experiences shape your understanding of what true love is?

~ How have past hurts or beliefs about yourself influenced your decisions and relationships? What steps can you take to rewrite those beliefs?

~ In what ways have you experienced the unconditional love of God? How has it transformed your self-worth and your relationships with others?

~ What does it mean to you to be "chosen, precious, and beloved" in God's eyes? How can this understanding influence your daily life and decisions?

*Stephanie*

# ABOUT THE AUTHOR

Stephanie Miller is an accomplished author, speaker, and certified Spiritual Growth Coach and Writing Coach, dedicated to empowering Christian women to embrace their creative potential. With a passion for inspiring others, she conducts live workshops, speaks at virtual events, and has been a featured guest on over 50 podcasts. Her published works include *The Butterfly Blueprint: How to Renew Your Mind and Grow Your Faith* and her most recent co-author book, *The Artist Haven: Fourteen Empowered Stories to Overcome Obstacles and Embrace Creative Expression.*

As the founder of Butterfly Beginnings Coaching LLC, Stephanie has guided numerous aspiring writers in overcoming their fears and honing their craft while deepening their faith. She shares her insights and wisdom on her Substack newsletter, "Live and Create Transformed by Butterfly Beginnings," covering topics related to motherhood, writing, creativity, and spiritual growth. She lives outside of Nashville, Tennessee, with her husband and three children.

**Find Me:**

Facebook: www.facebook.com/stephaniemillercoach

Instagram: www.instagram.com/stephaniemillercoach

Email: stephanie@butterfly-beginnings.com

Schedule a Call: https://calendly.com/stephanie-miller-hw/20-minute-discovery-coaching-call

# Courageous Voices Unlocked

*While I tried to fill a God-sized hole that only God could fill, my friend and co-author, **Amanda** found herself doing the same thing. Ultimately, she discovered God is her husband and provider. Her story is about how God replaced her shame with grace, His amazing grace.*

# DEDICATION

I dedicate my chapter to my amazing children, Lauren and Jackson. Thank you for making me a mother. It was My love for you that opened my heart to fully experience God's unconditional love for me. No matter what my accomplishments, being your Mom will always be the best thing I've ever had the opportunity to do!

Amanda Schaefer

# SHE LEFT HER JAR AT THE WELL

## Amanda Schaefer

Author, Speaker, Global Podcast Host

**Pennsylvania, USA**

*"Gratitude is the only proper
response to God's grace."*
~ Amanda Schaefer

When I got married the first time, I had no idea what to look for in a husband. I didn't know God, and I had grown up in a dysfunctional family where I saw more of a codependent relationship than a healthy marriage.

Because of this dynamic, I never understood boundaries. I experienced many traumas. I incurred wounds that never healed. I spent most of my life making horrible decisions, which led to even more trauma. I was utterly lost.

And yet, I did fall into what I thought was "love." I was married and had children, and now, all these years later—I live independently.

I was married twice. The first time, I married someone who didn't know how to lead me as a husband. I spent most of my time alone with my daughter and ended up getting divorced because I figured, why take care of two kids?

I was happy on my own with her. This was one of the best seasons I can think of. I loved her with everything I had, even though I was still very broken.

I married again and had my second child, who was nine years younger.

Having survived so many things but never having healed, my heart had built a wall around itself.

I ran away from complicated feelings—I ran to drugs or alcohol or promiscuity. I didn't know how to sit in the reality of my emotions—I didn't know how to heal. *I hadn't met Jesus.*

But God pursued me every single day, and one day, I heard Him. Although I grew up going, I no longer went to church. To me, it was just a building. I was in my home and heard God's voice. He pointed out something I was greedy and selfish, a truth I was trying not to see. In one instant, I agreed with Him, and miraculously everything changed.

Once I had accepted Christ, every part of me was different. I started getting up at five in the morning and going into my kitchen to pray out loud and to read a Bible I had never even opened before.

I started journaling, drawing, and worshiping, and my life bloomed. I started finding wisdom in the word of God, and I began to believe that God was for me and that I was His child. I was part of His family.

God grew me exponentially. Every time I went into His word, He showed me something new. I read every day, and a fire started burning in my soul.

About a week after I accepted Christ, my second husband started showing signs of being bipolar, and then he started self-medicating and became an alcoholic.

God was so kind to give me Himself to go to. God forged the foundation of my faith in those times of struggle. I had young children to care for, a home to try to keep, and the love of my life, Jesus, was there to hold on to.

Over the years, God has grown, molded, and pruned me. He has broken up the fallow ground in my heart and begun to sow harvest seeds for His kingdom.

My love for creativity came back: writing, speaking, painting, gardening, and decorating. Every part of my life showed a new joy; people saw it, and I always pointed to Jesus as the reason.

Although I had two earthly husbands with whom my marriages didn't last, I had never thought to ask God who I should marry, so this didn't surprise me. I didn't even think of God when I married them. I didn't ask if these were the people God had for me or if these would be good relationships, and God still blessed me with my precious children anyway. Two of my greatest blessings.

As I read the word more, I began to understand who God was; Jesus was my Husband, and I was not alone.

Isaiah 54:5 (ESV) says, *"For your maker is your Husband, the LORD of hosts is His name; and the Holy One of Israel is your Redeemer, the God of the whole earth He is called."* Somehow, I believed it.

## The Lord as My Provider

As time passed, there were occasions when I didn't have the money to pay my bills. After separating from my second husband, I had all the same bills and only half of the income.

In the Bible, God tells people to take care of widows and orphans, and in a way, I was a widow. My husband had left me emotionally way before he physically left our marriage. He was no longer in the role of husband. This man was mentally, emotionally, and spiritually absent. I was a widow raising children. That's how God saw me; He stepped in as my provider.

One day, I remember sitting at a little red table in my kitchen. I had all the bills in a stack on the table, and I would hold them up one by one in faith and say, "God, I can't pay this, but I trust you. Lord, this is your bill. I'm your wife; I'm your family. I trust you; you're faithful. Please take care of it."

As I held them up individually and spoke out loud to God, He heard me. *He paid them all.*

Another time, I had a new tax person go over my taxes, and the person who had done them three years before had missed something every year. It turned out that the IRS owed me $11,000 for those three years.

I received a check and cashed it. I must admit I waited a little while before spending the money because I feared the IRS would say, "Oh no, we made a mistake. Sorry, you owe us that money back." But time marched on, and that letter never came. God had done the impossible yet again. *When was the last time you heard of the IRS giving money back?*

Another time, I was in a small group for my church. I hadn't said a word to anyone, but I needed to pay a bill that I didn't know how I was going to pay. God must have spoken to these people. When I got home, I found several crisp $20 bills in my Bible and some more money in my pocketbook. My small group then was filled with young people who didn't have much money, but God had put it on their hearts to bless me.

And yet another time, I left my Bible at church by mistake. I ran to church the following Sunday looking for it. I looked in lost and found, and it wasn't there. I asked the pastor's wife, but she hadn't seen it. As a last resort, I returned to where I had been sitting the week before, and there was my Bible. I was so excited. I sat down for the sermon, and when we got to the book of Matthew, the part we were reading, I opened my bible and found it had money inside it!

God told people to bless me, and they blessed me. Psalm 50:10 (ESV) says, *"For every animal of the forest is mine, and I own the cattle on a thousand hills."* God owns everything. There is nothing in this world He cannot offer us. When God provides, we must remember He gives from a storehouse greater than any human can access. God owns everything!

God surrounded me with strong sisters and brothers in Christ and began providing a network of prayer warriors and encouragers to walk with me.

I remember feeling discouraged; without a husband I didn't have anyone to go to with my worries or problems. But God gave me a beautiful family in Christ. Men and women who I could count on. Sometimes, it was a provision as simple as a meal or a movie I could go to.

One time I was invited to the local beach for the day to sit in the sand and walk along the shore looking for seashells. This might not sound like much, but these things were empowering for me. I felt valued and loved. The Godly men in my life stepped up to be role models for my kids. The Godly women reminded me of who I was. Together, they edified and restored me and my children.

In 2012, I went on a mission trip to Malawi, Africa and spoke with the widows there. God gave me a specific message He wanted me to give them and a tangible thing that He wanted me to take them, but when I spoke with the people in charge of the mission trip, they said that I had to talk about their scheduled scripture instead.

I told them I would, but asked if I could please share what God had put on my heart because I knew it would be life-giving for these people. They told me I could do it if I could find a way to connect the two scriptures. I went to my prayer closet and asked God for His help, and of course, He provided a way.

I shared with these widows that same scripture from Isaiah 54:5 (ESV), telling them God, the maker of heaven and earth, was their Husband. I reminded them they weren't alone. In their culture, and in their country, if you don't have a husband or a son, you don't have anything. You can't earn money or own land.

As I told them God was their Husband and He would care for them and provide for their needs, I looked up for a moment, right into the longing brown eyes of the widow before me. She had deep wrinkles creasing her lovely face, most likely from a life filled with hardship. When she caught my gaze, her chin began to quiver. Slowly tears filled her eyes. They streamed down her cheeks. I felt my own eyes welling up with tears. And as if we had planned it, we both suddenly smiled. It was a moment I will never forget. Even though we didn't speak the same language or come from the same country, we saw each other. We knew each other's pain and happiness. Our hearts connected just like the ribbons we were braiding together with our hands.

I cut purple ribbons into strips and tied them into groups of threes at one end. I had my team members go among the women, and we each gave one of the widows the knotted end of the ribbons.

As they held them, we pulled back with tension, intentionally looking into their eyes and braiding the ribbon into one united strand we said, "This is how close God wants to be in your life." When we finished, we tied the now-braided bracelets of hope onto their wrists.

This is the same intentionality Jesus offered the woman at the well. She was alone with no one to help her too. She had no husband, "yet Jesus came close" to her. He looked directly into her eyes. He braided her life into His. He took her as His bride, filling her instantly with His eternal refreshment.

I was filled with encouragement and awe throughout our trip when we saw the widows in the villages walking around with their purple bracelets on. They were adorned in tangible reminders of God's love, presence, and provision, and confident of God's heart for them as their Husband.

Sometimes, I think it's ironic that God would use someone like me, someone who made my wayward choices.

I should have been an outcast in society. But God considers the giftings, talents, and passions that He intentionally deposited in me. They are precious jewels to Him.

Twenty-three years later, I have become a woman who preaches the Word of God. I am an evangelist in every sense of the word, using each opportunity to share about God's goodness. Since then, I have changed immeasurably more than I could have dreamed. I never would have imagined writing books, speaking on platforms, or producing and hosting a global podcast. I had been quiet for so long, hiding in plain sight the idea of speaking boldly to share the gospel everywhere would have stalled me in fear. Although I loved telling stories, I believed no one cared about what I had to say. God had different plans for my life.

To date, I have published two books of my own and have been published in two collaborative works. This is the third collaboration and I have one more slated to be published at the end of the year. Recently, I signed a contract to author a new traditionally published book of my own, expected to be released in February 2025.

I started a podcast that has become a global connection. I have shared it weekly for over three years, highlighting the stories of people who love the Lord.

I am the Samaritan woman filled with living water that bubbles up and overflows out of me. I'm continually running to tell everyone who will listen about my Jesus. I cannot fathom the kindness of a God who meets me in the arid afternoon desert as I stand alone, thirsty, hungry, and ashamed—a God who offers me more, who offers eternal and abundant life.

I need more than just being free for myself—I want everyone to be free!

The good news is this is not just for me, nor was it only for the Samaritan woman. She had no name on purpose so you and I could identify with her.

Jesus is willing to sit beside me and have an intimate conversation. He will meet me wherever I am. He doesn't come to shame me but to let me know He knows how I've been living and that He has a better way.

Jesus' grace, gentleness, and kindness brought me to where I am today. I speak about Him every chance I get, and I am grateful for His presence.

"Grateful" is a word many people use, but I believe gratitude is my only proper response to His grace.

I don't deserve to do what I get to do now, to be part of God's family or to be a highly favored daughter of the King. And yet, He loves me so immensely. He sees past my poor choices and sees straight to my heart, which He created many years ago.

He comes alongside me and continually pours Himself into me. I am refreshed and revived, ready to run into all the world and share His goodness. And so I go, running wherever I can with love in my heart and life in my bones.

When I consider who I was and how I lived my life before Christ, I can't help but think of the woman at the well.

The woman at the well is never named, yet her encounter with Jesus is the longest between the Messiah and any other individual in the Gospel of John.

She represented the lowest of the low in a society where women were both demeaned and disregarded. This woman was born of a race traditionally despised by Jews. She lived in shame as a social outcast.

One day, she has a Holy encounter with Christ and receives salvation. Ultimately, her testimony convinces an entire town to believe in Jesus. God turns her shame into joy;

an evangelist is born from a lowly sinner. This sounds much like my story!

I spent most of my life looking down, keeping quiet, and following the lead of whoever seemed the strongest in the room. I didn't realize the power I had available to me to speak and change the world around me because I kept my voice shut up and quiet deep inside of me. To go from never speaking unless someone talked to me to speaking out and sharing the gospel in boldness and strength no matter who was around me was the result of God's Holy Spirit flowing through me. Jesus made me new!

The presence of God's living water in a life revives it beyond the imagination! Everyone can see the transformation. What was old has been made new.

In those days, women typically drew water in groups in the morning before it was too hot. It was a social occasion. The fact that this woman was drawing water alone at midday indicates she was an outcast.

Interestingly, she felt comfortable talking with Jesus and asking him pointed questions. His answers to those questions and their ensuing dialogue reveal much more than surface conversation, adding significance to the story.

Jesus asked for a drink, and the woman wondered why Jesus could ask this of her as she was a Samaritan woman. She pointed out that Jesus had no cup and asked about this living water.

The woman began to speak on religious matters, noting that the Jews believed the place they had to worship was in Jerusalem. Jesus replied, "Woman, believe me, a time is coming when you will worship the Father, neither on this mountain nor in Jerusalem." (John 4:21 ESV)

No matter how much of an outcast we might be, God will intentionally come to meet with us. We are loved. He knows what He's poured into us. He knows who we are and will relentlessly pursue us until we turn to Him. We, too, can receive His living water.

The Samaritan woman came to the well at noon when it was too hot to draw water. Sometimes, I wonder if this is to show us her loneliness and deep thirst. Working to collect water in the desert at noon would undoubtedly make me thirsty.

She was there on purpose, knowing she would be alone. This woman was familiar with what the other women had to say about her, and she knew they were right.

She had heard about Jesus, and somewhere deep within her heart, every time she heard a story about what the God of the Israelites was doing, a tiny part of her began to believe, and layer by layer, that turned into a place of faith.

Jesus isn't about following man's rules. He's about following the laws of the Father. God's word says, *"You shall love the Lord your God with all your heart and with all your soul and with all your mind. This is the great and first commandment. And a second is like it: You shall love your neighbor as yourself"* (Matthew 22:37-39 ESV).

In His response here, Jesus challenges all our original ideas about who a neighbor was. He brought God's love directly to every person He encountered.

One of my favorite things about this story is where she started. She was thirsty and avoiding her troubles and the people around her, but once she encountered Jesus, fully revived—she ran back to tell others about Him.

This is who I am now, too. I return to where I started from, too. I speak boldly about Jesus. Filled with His living water, which splashes around me everywhere I go, quenching the thirst of hopeless, lonely sojourners in the desert. Every word of His truth I speak restores life.

Jesus knew everything about me, and He spoke to me. After Jesus revived me, just like the Samaritan woman, I told everyone I could about who He was.

The transformation at the well occurs when we are dry, and nothing the world can give us will restore and refresh us—only God, only the living water, only Jesus.

*"In Christ, my Life has a purpose*
*I never could have dreamed of"*
~ Amanda Schaefer

A Cup of Gratitude Ministries

*Amanda Schaefer*

The poem on the next page describes my relationship with Jesus. The way He loves me will always melt my heart.

## My Jesus

In the quiet of the morning,
I sit at your feet.
You teach me and adorn me
with your presence and peace.
I experience a filling deep inside my heart.
As you pour in living water,
and truth You impart.
As the dryness ceases and the overflow begins,
You gently remind me You have covered all my sins.
With one turn towards you,
and with genuine regret,
the death meant for me is forever reset.
You take the shame and torment,
You take the pain -
And you bear it with mercy and remind me it's slain.
What you accomplished cannot be reversed.
In relationship with you
I am eternally "un-cursed"
You call me your bride and prepare me for marriage.
You tend to my wounds and teach me love language.
The broken is transformed,
the empty is filled,
the forgotten is chosen,
the rejected, rebuilt.
The death that corrupted has turned dazzling white.
A bride and her Husband forever unite

# ABOUT THE AUTHOR

Amanda Schaefer is a storyteller at heart. Her greatest desire is to share the freedom she has found in Jesus. As an author, speaker, and global podcast host, Amanda comes alive recounting the goodness of God in everyday moments. The way she shares about the Bible makes it come to life. Amanda offers comfort and hope to those in difficult places. She desires to help everyone find moments of gratitude in the valley and places of light in the darkness. Her mission is to help people share their stories with the world so that they can ultimately share the stories God has written in their lives. Every story matters!

**Find Me:**

Facebook: www.facebook.com/amanda.f.schaefer

Instagram: www.instagram.com/acupof_gratitude

Website: www.acupofgratitude.org

Email: aschaefer40@gmail.com

Free Gift: https://bit.ly/3XOQzYs

# COURAGEOUS VOICES UNLOCKED

*Shame seems to be quite a common thread here, powerful, nonetheless. While I experienced shame for my past and who I was, the next co-author, **Teresa**, experienced shame brought on by her own mother for not living up to a certain standard. I invite you to read her story to find out how she came to embrace exactly who God has made her to be.*

# DEDICATION

This chapter is dedicated to Ernest McClure, my grandfather, who lived a vibrant life and made a commitment to extract "shine" in every life that he touched.

Teresa Dial

# SILVER THREADS OF REDEMPTION

## Teresa Dial

Author, Anxiety/Panic Coach, FinTech Professional,
Educator and Philanthropist

**Raleigh, North Carolina, USA**

*"For You, O God, have tested us; You have refined
us, as silver is refined"* (Psalm 66:10 NKJV).

### Silver's Refining Process

God is our master silversmith, and he does not waste the
fiery trials of our lives. He shapes, refines, and removes toxic
thinking or actions. He removes impurities and perfections
that are not like Him. Like silver, refinement challenges us to
*"shine,"* as we improve our *purity*, *worth*, and *ability to function*.
With a relationship with Him and a father's watchful eye, he
can protect us (safely) from injury and is willing to "take on
our heat." Our souls, like silver, must transfer heat (trials)
quickly back to Him to maintain proper function.[1] What God
wishes most is to see His own *reflection* when he looks at us.[2]
Further still, others should see Him in us.

Silver forged by fire, has much spiritual symbolism and
meaning to be gained in its refinement process. A shekel was
a unit of measurement to weigh metals for trade during
biblical days. Scholars believe that the earliest shekel used for
sacrifices in the tabernacle and for funding the tent meetings
were silver coins. The Israelites, both rich and poor, paid a
half shekel to God to atone for their sins.[3]

In Jewish culture, sages or rabbis of the past believe that when God gave instruction to Moses to have the Israelites pay, he was confused. God then showed him a half-shekel coin on fire for understanding. What God was conveying was that each coin represents holiness waiting to be released. When the shekel is paid cheerfully and for good use, it is the same as fire being released straight to heaven like a sacrificial animal. While a coin given with coldness and a grudge is not from the heart. God is concerned about our heart posture.[4]

*"The rich shall not give more and the poor shall not give less than half a shekel, when you give an offering to the* LORD, *to make atonement for yourselves. And you shall take the atonement money of the children of Israel, and shall appoint it* [exclusively] *for the service of the tabernacle of meeting, that it may be a memorial for the children of Israel before the* LORD, *to make atonement for yourselves"*
(Exodus 30:15-16 NKJV).

Silver is found as a compound mixed with lead and other metals, impurities and contaminants that must be extracted. When silver is refined it can go through any number of processes to remove imperfections and improve its purity. Results of these refinement are:

- **Purity** - it has a consistent composition which can be used for jewelry, coins, and industrial processes.
- **Value** - higher purity means higher market value.
- **Functionality** - refining maximizes the qualities it already has for maintaining energy, malleability, and corrosion resistance.
- **Safety** - since some impurities are toxic; refining removes them making silver safer to manage.

- **Reflectivity** - effectiveness in reflecting radiant energy and light.[5]

A silversmith is a skilled artisan who works with silver, crafting various objects and ornaments through techniques such as forging, casting, engraving, and polishing. Silversmiths often start with raw silver or silver alloys, then use specialized tools and techniques to shape and refine the metal into their desired forms. They may also incorporate other materials like gemstones or enamel to enhance the beauty and value of their creations.

*"But now, this is what the LORD says—he who created you, Jacob, he who formed you, Israel: 'Do not fear, for I have redeemed you; I have summoned you by name; you are mine"*
(Isaiah 43:1 NIV).

*"Comparison is the thief of Joy."*
~Theordore Roosevelt,
26th President of the United States

## Truth is Relative

Following the pandemic of 2020, many of us in the United States began to feel the effects of isolation, and extreme polarizing views on vaccines and social and political issues. This division was in addition to the culturally accepted norms that marginalize people based on their zip code, whether rich or poor, ethnicity, gender, and race. Furthermore, your social media profile and the number of followers is what determines social status, success and revenue potential in business and branding. All this stimulus continuously invades the psyche and covertly works to influence who you are or who you should be.

With the advance of Artificial Intelligence (AI) combined with social media, one can use filters and appear to be someone they are not and/or create an entirely realistic looking image or content that does not exist in the natural world. The journalism and media standards easily craft a story with little fact checking. The news is as good as the source that it originated from. This leaves society struggling daily to identify what is real and what is counterfeit?

Mental health issues are at an all-time high as people find themselves idolizing and obsessed with trying to measure their appearance and lifestyle against images and lifestyles of others. Many times, lifestyles are extremely embellished and/or fake. How does one protect their peace of mind from being bombarded with so much information that was never true to begin with? How does one prevent themselves from feeling and believing they will never be enough based on the images and lifestyles they see? How do we guard our minds from believing and accepting lies? All this information gives way to comparison and depression—the death of any personal joy one could have.

Today, the idea of truth is relative to the person speaking. Since no one is perfect and there is no absolute truth, it is based on your own individual standard and what you feel. It is therefore perfectly fine to speak half-truths or lie as needed. For those who dream of standing up for morals or God's truth, they find themselves being silenced by the majority. Encountering humans that define their own standards based upon the lies of society, influence, and comparison have been a source of major trauma in my journey and I imagine you also may have a similar experience.

*"All the carnal beauty of my wife is but skin-deep."*
~ Sir Thomas Overbury

One day, family pressure along with shame compelled my teenage mother to insist that I finish a bowl of cereal with strange blue capsules floating on top. The next thing I remember is screaming as hospital doctors forced a tube down my three-year-old throat to remove the pool of blue floaters at the bottom of my stomach! My mother wanted to rid me of existence and simply erase me. Man has always wanted to value people according to external and superficial traits such as looks or skin color. It is a total contradiction in how God views humans from an internal view. In 1 Samuel 16:7 (NIV) it says, *"But the Lord said to Samuel, 'Do not consider his appearance or his height, for I have rejected him. The LORD does not look at the things people look at. People look at the outward appearance, but the LORD looks at the heart.'"*

For me, my low value given by society is due to my dark skin color. Dealing with external racism is one thing, however, internal family racism or "colorism" is quite another. Man's faulty external valuation is what causes division and strife within my family. Many on my mother's side are mixed racially and range in skin color from white to medium brown. On my father's side, dark skin reigns. By the world's standards and my teenage mother, darker means "worthless and of no value" when compared to my sister.

My mother's family perspective is that they could not afford to degrade the family color standards. My father was deemed unsuitable, and the relationship ended as my mother found me to be a daily reminder of her "mistake" that must be eradicated. How can God find a silver lining in a situation in which one's own mother wants to erase you? The family's obsession with color is clearly a family generational curse or stronghold. How can God ever make use of those like me who are fed lies to believe we are mistakes and deemed worthless?

> *"For the LORD your God is he that goeth with you, to fight*
> *for you against your enemies, to save you"*
> (Deuteronomy 20:4).

Another trauma that affected me was a workplace issue with a newly hired boss within our team. Within one year, this manager carefully hand-picked areas that he could find to disrupt my world and/or try and force me to leave the company. As people were mandated to return to the office, I had obtained medical approval six months prior to be able to work from home. He made it his business to discredit it and demanded that records be reviewed again. The medical committee upheld the original decision and would not side with the manager to overturn it.

Later in the year, I received a new team offer from within the organization. After learning about it, he told the potential new manager that he was caught off guard about why I wanted to leave, and he would have to do more research. He was already aware of the hostility with business partners as the prior manager had briefed him on the subject when he came onboard. After weeks of stalling, the offering manager grew tired of waiting, rescinded the offer, and chose another candidate. The manager further decided he had yet one final trump card to play to erase me. When it came time for performance reviews, he made-up complete lies to deem me as "unsatisfactory" which would allow him to reduce my bonus compensation by 50% and stain my reputation.

What he failed to recognize was that I was a daughter of the King. I had no intention of retreating without a fight. I immediately submitted an HR investigation and dispute. Despite my brain being willing to fight, I found my emotions in a place of anger and depression. The anxiety and panic that I had long struggled with and had managed began to resurface. The familiar feeling of being on edge and dread waiting for something worse to happen was like a dark cloud following me around. Not much later came anxiety's cousin—a depression that was all-consuming. Depression for me is like the guest that never leaves, while anxiety comes and goes. Depression wanted permanent residency in my mind, which I knew I had to battle. During this time, I reminded myself of the power in just saying and repeating the name of Jesus until the darkness left me.

In Christian circles it is said that people who do not know Jesus, recognize someone who is of "the light" and they instantly find themselves not liking the person and not knowing why. Scriptures make it clear that we do not war with "flesh and blood," but instead war with powers of the dark and evil in the spiritual realm. The darkness was clearly acting as a puppet master directing this manager. How could God find a silver lining in this situation where a manager I had never met was hell-bent on slandering and terrorizing me? How does one fight a force wreaking havoc in your life that you cannot even see?

*"And we know that for those who love God all things work together for good, for those who are called according to his purpose"* (Romans 8:28 ESV).

## Finding My Own Personal Relationship with Jesus

In much of my early years, I spent time diligently trying to "make success happen" on my own. I had been in church my entire life, serving, tithing, teaching, helping the elderly and others in need. However, I had not fully experienced God one-on-one in my own life. I knew of Him intellectually, on paper, and as a God to my parents and others. I told myself I just needed to be persistent and eventually hard work would pay off. The problem is this approach works for many, but for others, it simply leads to the road of nowhere. It is a worldview.

In some cases, God simply will not let you do life without Him. Further, being a dark-skinned African American without connections, resources, or influence, it soon became clear that no matter how well-educated I was, nor how well dressed I was; I could not change the minds of society and those who had already predetermined my worth in this world.

One day, the Holy Spirit whispered to me these words: "You are trying to fight battles that you can never win." It was both shocking and irrefutable. I just had to accept this truth. I needed my own personal Jesus, who knows me. God wants to be personal and unique specifically for you. The best part is God does not measure or evaluate as man does and he can use people that do not fit the worldview, cliques, and cookie-cutter "success models."

Scriptures are clear that man's ways are not God's ways. On this earth, those who have "everything" materially – lack things that are "intangible." They cannot buy peace, love, joy, empathy, humility, nor salvation. Man's earthly superficial evaluation of himself and others is irrelevant when compared to God who prepares His eternal and final valuation based on the heart posture of every person.

I discovered that too much focus on oneself and "what is lacking" or ruminating on disappointments rather than being grateful for what we already have in hand leads to depression, anxiety, and fear. One way to solve this is to actively seek to make oneself useful by helping others, praying for, and serving others and actively seek gratitude. For me, my deliverance comes by soaking in worship music, scripture, random acts of kindness and a daily phone alarm reminding me to identify things to be grateful for.

When one focuses on the needs of others, they give their mind a break from being consumed by their own personal thoughts. Neuroscientists have proven that "depression" and "happiness" cannot exist at the same time in the brain. Which means you have the choice daily to choose happiness over depression. God has given the brain the ability to build new memories and new neural pathways to replace old ones. Once the peace of God is invited to indwell within you, you have a built-in support system to help guard your heart and mind. Activate His superpower to help attack what you lack!

As a result of this faulty valuation by society and family, I have learned to let God silver line my trials and use them for my good. I choose not to rely on social media and connections and people-pleasing for validation. In any fiery attack, my weapons are fasting, prayer with intercessory groups, communion, gratitude and scripture. Darkness cannot win against the praying daughter of the King and all the back-up firepower that comes from prayer groups. Darkness cannot win when God is sending direct commands to Michael and the other host of angels to wage war in the heavenlies. God has the final say!

I boldly declared to my manager, "My God would make his wrong decision *right*," and so it was! The senior executives met and agreed to "undo" all this manager had done, and he was subsequently shown the exit door! I pray that this manager and my family one day find a relationship with Jesus that is personal and unique to them. I pray they are shown how to live within God's higher standard.

## Loyal, Brave and True

In the Disney animated film, the Chinese story of Mulan, a girl, disguises herself as a male warrior to save her father from going to war. She wanted to honor her family and fight for their country. The lyrics challenged one to consider who they are without armor and standing in the shoes of their father? Are you capable of being strong or weak without your father near you? Lastly, underneath all the armor and deep within you, can you really be counted on to be loyal, brave and true?

Once we accept Christ, we become part of the "light," and must assume a warrior stance to fight against darkness and evil forces on this earth. In today's culture, anyone who decides to do what is right in ANY situation and challenges modern beliefs is mocked, ridiculed, erased and "canceled." It takes no special effort to just "go with the crowd" and live on lazy standards and lies. Being a warrior for Christ requires wearing the full armor of God and ready for battle in ALL areas of life. Do you compromise or hold fast and refuse to back-down from wrong ideologies, people, and threats? Are you a person of integrity that is loyal, brave, and true in ALL things? Can God count on you to share your trials with others and tell of His deliverance?

Many of us can recall memories as children walking in their parents' shoes. When we are emulating, we are like them, responding and behaving as they would. The enemy does not chase souls nor cause much trouble for those who have rejected Christ. He knows he has won them. Instead, he chases and wars with those that do not belong to him. Christ followers who he hopes will doubt and abandon the faith. Afterall, should it not be the understanding of the silversmith that designed us to determine our worth, understand our limits and identify what is required for us to function properly? A designer understands the composition of his work.

If you have not accepted Christ, the time is now. Just as God redeemed Israel, so shall he refine and redeem you. Your identity and worth do not have to be determined by the lies of society. You do not have to despair as you are more than enough! You do not have to rely on a man's endorsement alone for success. You do not have to embrace a life of brokenness and damage by others. You do not have to *take all the heat* alone. You *shine* when you tell your story and give God the glory. Rest knowing the master silversmith is in His studio, at work, designing a beautiful silver-lined redemption plan made specifically for you!

> *"But God hath chosen the foolish things of the world to confound the wise; and God hath chosen the weak things of the world to confound the things which are mighty;"*
> (1 Corinthians 1:27).

## Teresa Dial

Author, Anxiety/Panic Coach, FinTech Professional, Educator, and Philanthropist

I was inspired to write a poem on the next page titled, "An Ode to Life's Magnificent Paradox," to illustrate how living a life pleasing to the Father is the very opposite of human thought. Scripture makes it clear that His ways will not match ours. Often, He solves problems in ways that we were not expecting and He may ask us to do things that make no logical sense. Every day is a new adventure!

## An Ode to Life's Magnificent Paradox

What awe in nature that is forged by our Designer,
When there is ease for revenge only love must abound,
Only blessings and forgiveness for our oppressors,
Authority will not conquer instead a servant shall be found,
A mind fed on His word indeed starves fear and doubt.
Wealth sprouts in the heart when fortunes are poured out,
Lessen to become the center, all Glory goes to Him,
Care for the plight of others and thine own needs be dim.

# ABOUT THE AUTHOR

Teresa Dial is an Author, Fintech Professional, Philanthropist, Transformation Coach, and Owner of King's Heart Consulting. Her practice is dedicated to empowering clients on their healing journey, helping them break the chains of anxiety, renew hope, reclaim their lives, and rediscover their God-given purpose. For relaxation, Teresa enjoys harnessing the power of the pen, crafting, or listening to compelling storytelling. She is a passionate advocate for women's financial literacy, and children's advocacy and enjoys creating digital and social media content. She also enjoys music, singing, baking, and spending time in nature. Residing in North Carolina, Teresa takes delight in pampering her two fur children, a Norwegian forest cat named Heidi, and a black-and-white tuxedo cat named Mei Ling. Above all, her most significant work is being about her Father's business, and committed to seeking ways to change her small space in this world and leave it better than she found it.

**Find Me:**

Facebook: www.facebook.com/teresa.dial.167

Instagram: www.instagram.com/dial_boss23

LinkedIn: linkedin.com/in/tdialco

Email/Schedule a Call: dialteresa10@gmail.com

Free Gift for Client: Contact me via social media or email to receive your gift and include the words "Free TD24."

# REFERENCES

[1] Anne Marie Helmenstine, Ph.D., *What Is the Most Conductive Element?*, accessed on September 15, 2024, at https://www.thoughtco.com/the-most-conductive-element-606683

[2] Mr. Paul Thomson, *The significance of colours in the Bible: Silver*, accessed on September 15, 2024, at https://truthfortoday.org.uk/transcripts/T1026

[3] Rabbi Yechiel Eckstein, *Coin of Fire*, accessed on September 15, 2024, at https://www.ifcj.org/learn/holy-land-moments/daily-devotionals/coin-of-fire

[4] From the teachings of the Lubavitcher Rebbe; adapted by Moshe Yaakov Wisnefsky, *Silver Soul: Jewish mysticism teaches the powerful connection between opposing elements,* accessed on September 15, 2024, at https://www.chabad.org/kabbalah/article_cdo/aid/379880/jewish/Silver-Soul.htm

[5] Microsoft CoPilot, accessed on September 15, 2024. Prompt: "How is pure silver refined and extractions removed for the final product?" Generated using https://copilot.microsoft.com/

# COURAGEOUS VOICES UNLOCKED

*In discussing our worth and value to God, sometimes we must look beyond others' opinions and inwardly at ourselves. While I've dealt with my fair share of bullies, the next co-author, **Dorease**, is no stranger to bullying herself. She discusses how being bullied at work by the "coyotes" affected her and how she discovered "braveheart"—her courage within.*

# DEDICATION

With enduring depths of gratitude to Melissa, Missie, Michele, and more. You each portrayed immense character and bravery throughout those years. Thank you for linking your shield with mine…when you could've pretended you didn't know and didn't see.

For the lady warrior mentors in my life…my beautiful braveheart mother, Doris Haltom, and my sword-wielding "Colorado momma," Susan Skinner (who was promoted to Heaven months before this manuscript was published). Your unwavering love, prayers, and wise counsel reinvigorated me each time I became battle-weary.

And for others of you dragged into needless battles you never wanted, will you lean into the Lamb-turned-Lion-King Himself…draw on His strength…and invite Him to help you become strong and courageous, as well? I will be on castle ramparts cheering you on to victory.

Dorease

# FINDING BRAVEHEART
## INSPIRATION TO EMBRACE YOUR TRUE IDENTITY

## Dorease Rioux

The Victory for Purpose Coach

**Teller County, Colorado, USA**

*"Since it's so likely that children will meet
cruel enemies, let them at least have heard of
brave knights and heroic courage."*
~ C.S. Lewis, "On Stories: And Other Essays on
Literature"

I write this from battle-scars, not wounds.

Throughout the years, I've drawn inspiration from the courageous 13th-century Scotsman, Sir William Wallace, famously portrayed by Mel Gibson in the epic film, *Braveheart*. Wallace stood resolutely against brutal tyranny, fighting fiercely for freedom.

Over time, I, too, have yearned to rise up against injustice and oppression. I've learned a lot on the battlefield and become adept with sword and shield.

My wounds have become weapons for helping others. Thus, I hope what I'll share, regarding the pain of rejection, will inspire some of you toward a deeper healing journey with Jesus—The Messiah—The Anointed One.

## Playground Taunts and Tears

It was my first day at a school that was proud of their "Viking" mascot.

I was only ten years old… tall and willowy with long blonde hair. Because of my daddy's Scandinavian ancestry, I looked the part of a Viking child… because I was. Well, I was in part. In fact, I was merely a mutt medley, because I had some English, too, and my mother's lineage was mostly Scottish. Aye!

I wanted to fit in, brave little Viking girl or not.

In my one decade of life, I had been blessed to partake in sweetly affectionate friendships and had been cheerful and caring. As an encourager, I wanted everyone to feel liked, and their innate gifts celebrated. Thus, as a lassie, you could find me ever enlarging the circle around me as I sought to bless and build up others.

On this first morning in Viking-land, I didn't feel very brave. Instead, I felt unsettled. I hoped I would be accepted and find kind friends here.

At recess, I was approached by a cluster of four girls on the playground. The antagonistic ringleader targeted me immediately. She was blonde-haired, taller than me, and sturdy. Her whiskey-colored eyes were calloused to be so young, and so was her domineering personality. That first day, she commanded me to walk through green seepage water, climb up onto an old oak tree stump, hold a broken stick like a mic, and sing loud. The amused aggressor found great satisfaction in mocking me. The second day the demanding child ordered me to dance atop the once-grand tree. The third day, I made the mistake of mentioning that my sister and I had been away at charm school recently. Well, the taunting only intensified. And…so it went.

Although I wasn't weak, I was accommodating and had been taught polite Southern manners. So, the bully found ongoing ways to humiliate me. I felt shame for submitting to her heartless mistreatment. For two years, my dread to see her was like a dark cloud over my otherwise grateful, joyful heart.

I never told an adult about the troubled child's shenanigans but discovered precious friends in the other three girls who had been under her control, too.

## Whispers of Brave-Hearted Souls

My mother and paternal grandmother loved books and were voracious readers. I grew up with that same insatiable passion because storybooks enriched my soul.

During childhood, I was drawn to reading about bravehearted characters who overcame soul pain and disappointments, uplifted others, and regained confidence and courage. They helped me feel validated.

One such classic novel was *A Little Princess*. I understood Sara's heart from the first page to the last, and I amiably scrubbed floors at her side.

In *The Chronicles of Narnia*, I resonated deeply with the heart of Queen Lucy the Valiant. I buried my head into Aslan's mane and lion-strength came into me, too. I departed the woods by moonlight empowered as a lioness…for all of us had kingdom work to do.

In high school, I romanticized writing fairy tales that would inspire bravery to *"slay the dragon and take back the gold."* (That would become my motto in adulthood.)

I daydreamed about writing a Tony-award-winning script for a Broadway Show Musical that chronicled a painful story similar to mine: *"Brave Girl Triumphs Over Mean Girl."* However, in reality, I hadn't prevailed over my fear of domineering personalities, and I still wore a cumbersome sign around my neck that read: *"Easy Target for Bullies!"*

Fear of rejection triumphed over the wanna-be-brave Viking girl, and it would be a long while before I'd learn about spiritual weaponry, how to armor up, and would muster courage to descend from the safety of castle ramparts to prove my mettle on the battlefield.

## Forged in the Fire

I experienced firsthand that the silent suffering of innocent people is real. I learned we live in a natural, fallen world where satanic agents are on assignment to wreak havoc…and that other people have free will to yield to and unknowingly be used by the enemy, especially if they aren't walking close with the Lord and staying tuned in to the voice of the Holy Spirit every day.

In spite of letting fear hold sway throughout my adolescence, I grew up with a tender heart for the things of God. I thirsted to read my Bible every day and was reassured by passages like Psalms 23, 27, 91, and others.

I often personalized and proclaimed Joshua 1:9 and was drawn to courageous Bible characters like Joseph and David. I resonated with their persevering faith in the thick of rejection. They were Bravehearts forged in fire and both left behind a rich legacy!

## A Resurgence of Confidence and Courage

As a young woman, I fell prey to further soul-pain injuries in a destructive relationship with a controlling and abusive one-person-wrecking-crew. In that crazy-making cataclysm of betrayals, jealous raging, and cleverly convincing deceits, I suffered silently and, when I was ready, the Lord helped me escape.

Soon thereafter, I left bedside nursing as a critical care RN, too, as I catapulted into a dynamic industry for over 20 years where I flourished and thrived, and was still able to impact patients' lives as a nurse.

I worked hard and smart. I lived with an enormously grateful heart before the Lord every day and knew He had blessed me to be a blessing. So, that further enriched the joy I experienced on this exciting career path with countless noteworthy accomplishments.

I never took anything for granted. I marveled with humility and glorified God as His blessings seemed to chase me down and overtake me, year-over-year.

I became a successful businesswoman, known for my positive can-do attitude and integrity, thus, my reputation in Corporate America was noteworthy. And, as a visionary leader and supportive team-player, I was valued and appreciated…until…I wasn't.

## Hostile Horizons

After a long stint with that one extraordinary company, I went to another esteemed organization in the industry.

My first day on the job was at a company-wide meeting. With hundreds of employees milling around a spacious concourse, two particularly contemptuous team-members came solo to introduce themselves. When the high-energy one approached me, her eyes flashed, and her seething-fury flared. She proclaimed with sneering indignation that she understood I had been in management at my previous company, and if I became a manager at this one, she would never work for me.

Bam! Just like that, she "put the new girl with the 'yes' face in her place." She threw back her head with a devious cackle and slithered away to gloat. She might as well have screeched: "I'm going to get you my pretty…and your little dog too!"

That brash-and-bitter bully was antagonistic and quick-witted. She was celebrated and cemented in like a golden goose…while her sour-and-dour, equally sarcastic sidekick was like a stink bomb in the room.

My new boss was a nondescript woman, a weak people manager, and a puppet for her boss. She enabled the brash-and-bitter bullies and misused the performance appraisal system. I met and exceeded my company-set goals every eligible year, but my annual performance ratings were given the bare bones, and my pay raises the bare minimum. There was false cordiality, undermining, and manipulations aplenty.

Then there was her boss. He was a compact little man on a power-trip with false humility and an enormous ego. He was longtime friends with the brash-and-bitter bullies. For eight years he abused his position of authority over me, while I repeatedly earned the right to receive a promotion within the franchise. Without explanation, he never gave it to me.

The four of them banded together early on with a mob mentality and marked me for takedown. They didn't care about the pain they caused but seemed to feed on it.

## Light Over Darkness

In John 10:10, we're told that satan comes to steal, kill, and destroy. It's his mission statement. And this foursome seemed to be influenced by the demonic. I doubt they even knew why they resented me, nor that they were allowing the devil to use them to batter a beloved daughter of the King.

It was a clash between light and darkness. Clearly, the light of Christ in me was too bright for them. My shine revealed the tarnish of their souls. They didn't like that; thus it didn't make it easy for me.

## Grit and Grace in Adversity

I never adopted a victim mindset at any point in my life. I never wanted anyone to feel sorry for me. Sure, I enjoyed attention, but only for positive things, not for negative reasons.

I vacillated between advancing in faith one day then shrinking back in fear the next. It was my portrayal of a Highland Dance with two steps forward, and three steps back.

I was determined to live from a place of victory—even as my cortisol levels from chronic stress weakened my immune system and the opportunistic spirochetes of Lyme Disease stuck up their ugly heads a few months after I joined the company.

At the time, we didn't know it was Lyme. My internist thought it was fibromyalgia, but every day that underlying tick-borne illness made me feel like I had the worst case of a flu virus…with immense fatigue, weakness, all-over achiness, and joint pain.

Nonetheless, I never once complained or called in sick. I never even told my company I was ill. With my severity of Lyme, the healthcare professionals said I should've either been bed-bound or bedridden. Over the years, they were bewildered that I could walk into their clinic every other week as they managed my care.

Against the odds, I did my job proficiently and my annual results proved I was a consistent top performer. This wasn't because I was "Wonder Woman," but because I leaned heavily on the Lord who helped me and I was empowered by His grace, which was sufficient each day.

## Courage Under Siege

Early on, the foursome had seemingly shape-shifted into a pack of ever-cunning and conniving coyotes. I was like a defenseless champion barrel-racing horse in a corral with some wily brutes.

I'm self-aware that I have faults and shortcomings. I readily admit them, and the Holy Spirit and I work on them. However, to be unjustly targeted and oppressed for no valid reason seemed villainous.

It might've been easier to comprehend if there had been a logical reason. However, I couldn't understand their game-playing and why they were threatened by me. I was an ideal employee. I made the company look good. I modeled depth of character. I was coachable. I did everything I was instructed to do and more. I was respectful of everyone. I was trusted and appreciated by my other colleagues at every level, as well as by my customers in my assigned healthcare systems and hospitals.

These things seemed to frustrate the coyote pack even more.

Honorable leaders with true integrity would've been thankful to have a competent, diligent, and strong account manager and team-player like me. They were not!

## Battle-Weary Resilience

I desired to please God. I stayed intimately connected with Him, kept my heart clean, and encouraged others. I only grew closer to the heart of the Father…the opposite of what satan had intended.

At work, I yearned to feel valued, safe, and secure, but to even hear their names mentioned brought knots to my stomach. I experienced chronic worry with ruminating thoughts that caused restless sleep patterns and sleeplessness.

I was so overly cautious that I would spend an hour re-working my emails and voicemails to inspire softer responses. I cringed to receive a message from one of the coyotes or to hear my boss' obnoxious ringtone. I dreaded conference calls, team meetings, and having to be in the same place as the undermining coyote pack.

I grieved over the diminishing of some closely held core beliefs, too. I had expected managers in this industry to be respectable, to reward hard-working personnel who put the numbers on the board, to be pleased to have employees with positive attitudes, for mean-spirited team-members to be held accountable, and for everyone to be treated fairly. I grieved those expectations, and so much more, that were stolen from me. On top of that my self-esteem was being affected.

Quietly battling against chronic Lyme Disease, trying to stay unnoticed, strategically driving my business, and managing the second-heaviest travel geography in the USA… were each enormous stressors that left me drained.

Surprisingly, I still loved my day-to-day job that didn't directly involve them. Thus, I refused to let the coyote pack steal it from me, and every year the Lord prepared a table before me in the presence of my enemies.

Overall, I cherished my time at home on the ranch with Tim, our dogs, and horses. I delighted in reading, creative writing, wonder-walk-about hikes in nature, co-creating with Elohim, and artistically expressing my 'innate good eye' in various ways.

## The Cost of Silence

Although I knew my integrity carried a lot more weight than their titles and opinions, as a lifelong "Pollyanna" optimist, I hoped they would stop the heartless nonsense, thus, I hung in there for eight years because of that lucrative job I was energized by.

Periodically, my precious mother, who had encouraged me to "kill them with kindness" and to "cultivate the fruit of the Spirit", reminded me that she had raised me up as a Southern Belle, with impeccable manners and good etiquette, who could trust God. She believed I was being Christ-like and honorable to keep turning the other cheek.

Some esteemed colleagues pleaded with me to document everything, respectfully push back, and/or open a case in Human Resources. A few nudged me to leave the job and consult with a corporate attorney.

Maybe everyone was right, but I graciously produced more good fruit and forgave each transgression.

Of course, I should've stood up for myself, but I was shackled in fear because the bad players were entrenched. They knew people.

So, the coyote pack got away with their many misdeeds.

I'm not sure which was worse for me: *The cost of silence or the weight of endurance.*

## Defying the Darkness

It was easy to 'lay down self' each day to yield to the Lord, and to esteem others more highly than myself. Since girlhood, I had never needed to have power or control over anyone. So, when someone exerted prideful arrogance, jealousy, malice, and/or manipulations against me, it caught my attention because I wasn't wired to treat others that way.

When I was a wee lassie, demonic spirits had certainly realized I had been born as an encourager to refresh and empower others. The easiest way to derail my destiny story would be to target my self-esteem with rejection, betrayals, and/or abandonment. Thus, throughout my journey, the enemy had leveraged some deeply troubled people to spitefully begrudge and selfishly work against me and my true identity.

Those massive assaults had been hurled at the core of who I am, thus my achievements through the years had proven battle-wrought and hard-won.

## Turning the Page

During my final year there, I had been tracking #1 out of 144 account managers. I completed the year with my head held high and left the coyote pack foursome behind.

I forgave and gave up my right to harbor offense…I didn't want any trace of it in my heart. And as unnatural as it was, I still prayed for them, realizing I might be the only one who ever did. Also, I'm not a vengeful person and didn't even partake in an exit interview. Instead, I gave several weeks' notice and quietly departed.

It was liberating to turn the page and begin a fresh chapter.

That same month, I met with two ministry leaders. Those two women and I shared, prayed together, broke off a tag-along spirit of fear from my life, then we closed and sealed that door. Since that August day, I've never again felt fear of coyote-type people.

## Unveiling Braveheart

A few years later, on a beautiful summer day, I went to sit outside on our secluded mountain top. I had my Bible and a cup of coffee for my "Java with Jehovah" time. I was immersed in the awe and wonder of the birdsong, crisp mountain air, and beauty all around. I praised and prayed, but shame began to surface that I had tolerated the behaviors of some self-serving, entitled individuals over the decades and allowed them to get away with their wrongdoings against my heart.

As I reflected and prayed in the Spirit, I placed my shame on the altar, renounced it, and covered it in the blood of Jesus. I knew when shame lifted from me.

The Lord led me to Psalm 37, and I read it with unveiled eyes. My loving Heavenly Father helped me see He had fashioned me with 'staying power.' He spoke to my heart that 'it had taken a strong and courageous Braveheart to daily yield before Him, trust, obey, forgive, and not run away.' This epiphany was a gift to my heart. How had I not seen myself like this until today?

I envisioned how I was strong and courageous like Joshua, Caleb, and the illusive Mountain Lions that roamed our ranchland forests. The Lord helped me see I had never been weak-of-soul because it's a deeply insecure person that won't rationally handle opposition. That's especially true if they're inherently prone to defensiveness, blame-shifting, excuses, and denial. I never had been. In contrast, it had taken confident inner-strength and courage to endure in faith like Aslan's lion-hearted Lucy…and me.

As a Braveheart, I arose to stand up tall that morning on the mountain. I felt awe-struck over our majestic view of the Pike's Peak Mountain range, realizing I had always been braver than I felt.

Over time, I had begun to align with God's banner over me, for His perfect love had cast out fear. I had, finally, embraced my supernatural identity as a Daughter of the Most High King.

I now agreed with what the beautiful Holy Spirit revealed. I had been tenderly fashioned for love, not fear…for acceptance, not rejection…and for honor, not shame. He had helped me emerge 'out of hiding' to shine bright and re-ignite my creative and colorful flair for life that some had sought to eclipse. I had moved forward with my gifts and calling, to fulfill my destiny story with divine purpose.

## Reclaiming My Power

The same week the spirit of fear was broken off, I had decided I would no longer tiptoe around toxic people, but would take back what the enemy had stolen—my power and my voice.

Practically speaking, if I were to do it differently today—I would still be politely-gracious to coyote types, but 'nip it in the bud' early on, respectfully push back, and firmly stand up for myself.

I would stay more vigilant to take up my spiritual weaponry and utilize warfare tactics against evil spirits. And I wouldn't allow fear-laden feelings to steer me toward isolating and trying not to stand out, but would shine like a city on a hill.

If I would've set a firm boundary line in place at 10 years old, in that former destructive relationship as an adult, and with the workplace foursome later, I might've prevented lengthy seasons of silent suffering.

When we remain in toxic environments, our self-esteem can become blurred, and our true identity takes dangerous hits. Thus, it's vital that we become clear on 'who we are in Christ.' It'll keep us rock-steady when our beliefs and personalities get hammered.

God never meant for His children to merely survive, but to know our true identity so we could flourish and thrive, no matter what.

## True Identity Embraced

Rejection, as well as betrayal and/or abandonment, is prone to foster an identity crisis if we don't already understand who we are. Jesus addressed identity in Luke 4. He wants us to center our identity in Him. I had thought I knew that. I preached sermons about identity. However, for too long I had cared too much about what others thought of me.

However, as I began to agree with who God says I am in scripture, the opinions of people mattered less. I discovered that my true worth isn't based on what other people "think" of me, but my value is anchored in what God "knows" about me. Jesus put His Name in me and on me. I am His. As a result, I've gradually learned not to attach myself to my achievements, titles, financial status, ancestral lineage, nor to others' opinions of me.

I choose to *'lay myself down'* at His altar everyday as I submit to Jesus and resist the devil. Moreover, it's a precious privilege to praise, worship, and pray in the Spirit…and to tune in to the good Shepherd's voice. I feast in and decree God's Word over myself, my family, and circumstances. I renew my mind in Ephesians, Colossians, and other passages which have become signature treasures in my life. I armor up and take up the shield of faith against all the fiery darts of the evil one and wield the sword of the Spirit which is God's Word. I believe God is Who He says He is. And…I continually embrace the redemptive truth of who He says I am.

I recaptured who God originally designed me to be, with a bold new confidence, for my true identity is found in the Lord Jesus…in God's lavish love for me as His beloved daughter.

As followers of Christ, we are all in the royal family! And He beckons each of us toward a lifestyle of freedom, but it's our choice to "give Jesus our best yes" to embark on that road less traveled by.

## A Call to Freedom for a Battle-Scarred *Lioness*

The Lion of the Tribe of Judah…majestic and mighty…has triumphed over sin, death, hell, and the grave. His name is Jesus. He's my Savior, Lord, and Redeemer… who invested His precious, powerful, royal blood in me. I'm *a daughter of The King* of kings. He called me to rule and reign with Him, forever and a day.

I may still be a Scottish Viking girl, but my genetic history is no longer what defines me. My true identity is rooted deeply with who I am in Christ. I'm like *a battle-scarred, lion-hearted lioness,* entrusted with His name, power, and kingdom authority to roam the earth with the Good News. With His heart of enduring strength, confidence, and courage, I no longer lose sleep over the schemes of coyotes.

I found Braveheart! He's Jesus the Warrior King. He's the Commander of the Lord's army, and I ardently follow Him. *As a braveheart lady warrior,* I serve under His command. I choose to live from a place of victory as I partake in God's divine nature.

It's your call to freedom, as well. I beseech you to join me on this wondrous kingdom adventure where you're accepted in the beloved and can leave fear behind… where brave-hearted faith lights the path for healing from rejection…and where the eternal story of the Lamb-turned-Lion King unfolds in ever-greater glory.

The victory Jesus won can become the strongest, mightiest roar over your life, too.

Beholding Him,

**Dorease**

*"When you are pursued by shadowy characters, who seek to eclipse your radiant light, know it's not a sign of your weakness; but a testament to the profound brilliance and beauty they see inside you. So, hold steadfast to your faith and true identity, with confidence and courage, and go forth as a lion-hearted Braveheart who shines bright, like a beacon in the night, inspiring and guiding others, as you set your path aflame for the glory of God."*
~ Dorease Rioux

~ If in the wink of an eye you could turn off a hindrance that holds you back, what would it be?

~ What would that be worth to you?

~ How would your life improve?

# ABOUT THE AUTHOR

Dorease Rioux is known as a cheerleader for dream chasers and dream-doers! As "The Victory for Purpose" Coach, Dorease empowers other kingdom-minded Christian women with how to achieve break-through from hurts that hinder and hold them back…AND…to discover and step into their God-given purpose so they can fulfill their destiny story with a bold new confidence.

After leaving her plane-hopping, award-winning career as a corporate executive, Dorease founded "Crowned for Purpose Enterprises." She's an entrepreneur, a #1 International Bestselling author, and a dynamic speaker with messages that are relatable and change lives.

Dorease and "The Amazing Tim Rioux" enjoy their country-living lifestyle with seven beloved dogs and a myriad of other delightsome creatures great and small. Dorease tends well to their animals with lots of TLC, singing, and camera clicks as a longtime wonder-graced shutterbug.

**Find Me:**

To schedule a free 30-minute "Victory For Purpose" coaching call with Dorease, send a direct message via Facebook Messenger.

Facebook: www.facebook.com/dorease.rioux

Private Facebook Group:
Wear the CROWN. Fulfill the CALL.
https://www.facebook.com/groups/529654824795621

YouTube Channel: Crowned for Purpose.
https://bit.ly/4eszmte

LinkedIn: www.linkedin.com/in/dorease-rioux-a013938

On Amazon, you can find international best-selling collaborative book projects with Dorease's published works:

~ The Artist Haven
~ Jim Britt's Cracking the Rich Code, Volume 11
~ Dear Superwoman
~ Take Your Position

# COURAGEOUS VOICES UNLOCKED

*Understanding your identity in Jesus Christ is a profound journey. When you yield to Him and embrace who you truly are, it can lead to life-changing mindset shifts. Our next co-author, ShonaRobyn, shares a heartwarming story of courage, as she moves from abandonment to being reunited with her birth mother. A powerful story of redemption and purpose,* **ShonaRobyn** *highlights the everlasting hope we have as children of God.*

# DEDICATION

This chapter is dedicated to my beloved grandsons, my children, my multiple families, and those friends who chose love and forgiveness during my tumultuous Camino of Life.

I am eternally grateful.

To Lachlan, Saxon, and Brody my Grandsons,
Life is a miracle,
Every day.
You are a miracle,
Every day.
Navigate your miracles,
Every day.

Love, Adventure Nan ShonaRobyn xx

# LOST AND FOUND
## ADOPTION: A JOURNEY OF PAIN AND MIRACLES

## ShonaRobyn Eisenberg

SR Restoration Life Coach

### A New Zealander Living in Sydney, Australia

*"And not only that, but we also glory in the tribulations, knowing that tribulations produces perseverance; and perseverance, character; and character, hope"* (Romans 5:3-4 NKJV).

### My Painful and Miraculous Start to Life

I am the baby born to an unmarried mother in 1948. A painful start to life for a newborn baby, coming straight from the comfort of my mother's womb to aloneness. And silence.

Alone in a maternity ward cot. White sheets. White walls. White ceiling. No colour. No mother. No comfort.

Lost and alone.

It would be many, many years before the pain within my broken heart would be recognised as grief, because this lost and alone baby had no way, nor no one, to recognise or share her pain. A pain which would dictate my life and my relationships into my older years.

In this era, the unmarried mother, pregnant with an illegitimate baby, was the source of great shame for her family. The societal pressure of the day was for the illegitimate baby to be relinquished into adoption. Anaesthetised during her delivery process, my birth mother woke in the maternity ward, alone, surrounded by married mothers with their babies in their arms.

Numb with trauma and grief, she signed the adoption order placed in front of her by the social worker, named me "Robyn" on the birth certificate, and left the ward.

However, this traumatic moment in her life journey as an unmarried mother, masks the miracle that occurred in the final weeks of her pregnancy, when my heavily pregnant birth mother left the tobacco fields of Marlborough Sounds to return to Wellington city.

Miracle for her. Miracle for us. Orchestrated by God…His purpose and plan over our lives.

Abandoned by her family, my birth mother had left her home and made her way to Marlborough Sounds in New Zealand's South Island, during the tobacco picking season to try and earn enough money to keep her illegitimate baby. Sadly, the season ended leaving her with very little money, unemployed, no available pension, and very pregnant.

Her decision to board the inter-island ferry and return to Wellington city reveals the miraculous Hand of God covering our lives. To appreciate the significance of this moment you must understand that my birth mother had been without her own mother since she was three years old. The scourge of cancer had taken her mother's life at the early age of thirty-three, leaving her war veteran husband widowed and alone, to raise his toddler aged daughter and son. They both had their share of hardships in their lifetime.

Disembarking from the inter-island ferry, alone, financially broke, and spiritually heartbroken, my birth mother stopped a stranger walking towards her, to ask for directions to the Salvation Army soup kitchen.

The stranger stood still, staring intently at the pregnant young woman in front of her. "What is your name child?" she asked.

"Beryl Wallis," my mum replied.

The stranger gasped and then introduced herself. "I am Mrs. Dixon," and taking a deep breath she explained, "I was a bridesmaid at your mother's wedding. I was her best friend. You are coming home with me."

The relief experienced in that miracle moment could never be measured. Mrs. Dixon was no stranger. Mrs. Dixon was a gift from God placed in that Wellington city street to meet her best friend's daughter in her hour of desperate need. What an extraordinary miracle for Beryl and me. Grandmother Olive Wallis, deceased for sixteen years, watching over her daughter and soon-to-be-born granddaughter, bringing us together with her beloved friend. If my cup of gratitude overflowed when my birth mother shared this story with me, how would my birth mother have been feeling at that moment? When the complete stranger standing before her not only recognises her—but takes her home? Love and loving kindness prevail. God, and only God, could create that fateful meeting of these two strangers in the streets of Wellington on that day.

My birth mother spent the final weeks of her pregnancy in Mrs. Dixon's home, in Lower Hutt, being loved and nurtured. And for Beryl, that haven would continue for the months that followed my birth and relinquishment. A safe place. Calm and Caring. No judgement. Her haven, until she left on her wedding day to build her future family of four more children.

**The Miracle of Leaving the Nursery**

I was demonstrating classic infant failure to thrive syndrome, losing weight, and withdrawing from the world.

Alone in my silent world, I wondered "Does anybody care for me?" "Will anyone love me?" Silent babies concern the staff looking after them. Newborn babies are not supposed to be silent. A newborn baby is a bundle of noisy demands!

Finally, the chosen couple (Duncan and Norma MacLean) were advised there was a baby girl waiting for them in the Lower Hutt maternity ward. My adoptive father would tell me how the phone call from the hospital social worker came to him at the Bank of New Zealand, where he worked. In 1948, he did not own a car, nor did they have a telephone at home. Overjoyed with the news, he first had to seek permission from his manager to leave the office during business hours. Once permission was granted, he then jumped on his bicycle and rode home at breakneck speed to tell his wife, "We have a daughter!" Not many men have the opportunity to break that news to their wife and baby son.

Once again, the Hand of God provided the connection to bring about the next miracle over my life. Her name was Betty Cook. Charge Sister, Lower Hutt Hospital Maternity Ward. Betty Cook recognised my adoptive mother walking towards her as a professional colleague—they had been student nurses at Wellington Hospital in 1940. Student nurses together during the horrors of WWII. Whilst they never left the shores of New Zealand to the front lines of the war, the war came to them. The wounded soldiers, shell shocked, maimed, crippled, blinded, limbless, and shockingly scarred burn survivors from tanks and warplanes. The hospital ships coming from the war zones of North Africa, Europe, and the Pacific, brought the horrors of war home to New Zealand, to the nurses and medical teams of Wellington Hospital.

Betty Cook and Norma MacLean had bravely shared those horror years.

In that moment of recognition, Betty Cook was able to make a professional decision, only she could make when she decided I was going home.

The professional practice of the day was that all newborn babies had to make up their birth weight before they could be discharged home. Concerned, Betty Cook, knew that was not going to happen for me.

When sharing my adoption story, my adoptive mother would speak of how Betty Cook wrote my new name on my discharge papers, bravely wrote my discharge weight as healthy and acceptable, dressed me in my going home clothes, then placed me in my mother's arms, speaking softly.

"You must take Shona home now. She is not going to make it here."

Medically and legally, a professionally risky decision, which may have saved my life. I am not sure if such a decision could happen in the modern era of nursing, I only know that such moments in my birth/adoption story are precious beyond measure. When God says, "I will never leave you, nor forsake you," (Hebrews 13:5) He is speaking to me. He is the anchor in the challenges I faced at birth, and the orchestrator of my amazing, adventurous life which will include reunion with my beloved birth mother forty years later.

**New Zealand—Glorious and Beautiful**

And God placed me, geographically, in one of the most beautiful countries on this earth—New Zealand. My adoptive father is a troubleshooter for the Bank of New Zealand, a man of integrity, employed to keep the banks honest.

After such a challenging start to my life, my childhood years are then taken up with changing towns and changing schools. I learned to love this gypsy lifestyle. I loved every move. I learned to move forward and never look back. I learned to travel alone.

I was ten years old when the very best of my life experiences came my way, thanks to New Zealand's Southern Alps. My adoptive father had been transferred from the North Island to Christchurch (in the South Island). He had been invited to bring his family to Glenthorne Sheep Station, in the heart of our glorious Southern Alps.

Always a sufferer of terrible car sickness, the first car trip to Glenthorne Sheep Station was a blur of nausea and wanting to throw up. I remained curled up in a ball in the back seat of the car—a 1958 Morris Oxford—the smell of back seat petrol fumes adding to my misery.

As instructed, my father stopped at the ranger's homestead overlooking Lake Coleridge. I knew exiting the car promptly would relieve my misery. I fell out the car door, eyes tightly closed, trying not to throw up.

The moment my feet touched the ground, I was blindsided by the most extraordinary blast of freezing Antarctica air filling my lungs and slapping my pale face. Every cell in my body erupted into a state of bliss as I was visually astounded by the gloriously beautiful snow-covered mountains surrounding Lake Coleridge, and me, for the first time.

This was the breathtaking presence of God over my life, the awesomeness of His creation filling my senses, and the Antarctica wind His comforting touch.

I will spend my life seeking to recapture this moment. Seeking the wind in my face, and always finding it. Regardless of my circumstances, regardless of how fast I ran, regardless of how far I travelled—God would never leave me, nor forsake me.

## Understanding My Adoptive Parents—Understanding Me

I came to realise the significance of this experience, the reason for God's comforting touch in the wind, when I recognised my behaviours in adulthood. In the post war years returned soldiers and their families resorted to stoicism to cope with their PTSD. This was a universal belief for survivors of the two world wars. My adoptive father had served in the Pacific campaign. My adoptive mother was a WWII nurse. Parents surviving their own WWII experience believed in raising their children "tough." It was an integral part of surviving.

My adoptive mother told me how a newspaper article in the early 1950's influenced their child-raising beliefs. They had read these comments, and embraced them:

"Do not hug the child, you will spoil them."
"Do not praise the child, you will spoil their ego."

So, my adoptive parents raised my older brother and I without hugs, cuddles, nor praise. No matter the circumstances we were experiencing, including the death of my favourite grandfather, or my friend who drowned when I was ten years old, my adoptive mother kept her distance, shared the tragedy, and walked away. We were not invited to healthy discussion, to have an opinion, nor was emotional engagement allowed. We were raised within tight tribal rules of silence and secrets, enforced by my long-suffering adoptive mother's relentless anger. Anxious for safety, I lived my life in a state of permanent dissociation—disconnected from myself, and from those around me. So long as I could feel the touch of the wind, I felt alive and loved. Love presented itself every day in the beauty in my surroundings.

I grew up with no awareness of how to build intimate relationships, nor how to engage in intimate conversation. Those skills came later through therapy and Life Coach courses.

My childhood therapy was visual, in the breathtaking beauty of New Zealand's glorious Southern Alps, and feeling God's Presence in the touch of the wind in my face. I was comforted, and my entrenched spirit of adventure ensured I was never lost and alone in the great outdoors.

## Yearning for Connection 1988

It was forty years before the yearning to find my birth mother surfaced within me. New Zealand changed its Adoption Laws in 1985 to encourage reunion among the 80,000 registered adoptions in New Zealand's population of four million citizens.

With two children now aged seven and five, somewhere deep in the core of my being came the realization my children cannot be left not knowing who they are, disconnected from their identities and biological heritage like their mother. Disconnected from my own needs, the initial driving force for reunion was to protect my children. Then, as I wrote my introductory letter, and collected photos to accompany that letter, I became aware that I really wanted to meet my birth mother.

Suddenly, after forty years of genealogical bewilderment (identity confusion), avoidance, and denial, there was a hunger, a yearning to know who I was, who my mother was, where she was, and how she was doing. I wanted to let her know how grateful I was for the life, and life experiences, her sacrifice had given me. I wanted her to see for herself my husband, (George Eisenberg) my children, and the extraordinary life I was living. This sudden, momentous decision came out of left field, like my favourite Antarctic blast, and would take me on the emotional and psychological ride of my life.

## Receiving My Original Birth Certificate in 1988

The first revelation of biological identity came with applying for my original New Zealand Birth Certificate.

This is a unique experience for adult adoptees who have no prior knowledge of their birth names, nor the names of their biological parents.

Just receiving this information is an emotionally charged experience. To finally learn that I was named at birth by my birth mother, and to read her name for the first time. Exciting. Breathtaking. Overwhelming.

My Birth Name: Robyn Elaine Wallis

My Mother's Name: Beryl Frances Wallis

This was such a significant moment in my adoption journey. It takes weeks to psychologically and emotionally absorb this new information. There are no shortcuts through this process as the brain rewires itself to new information and new identity. Anxiety prevails when facing such uncertainty, and such an unknown future. *Joy or rejection? Happiness or heartbreak?*

And I had not yet met my birth mother. That event took place six months after I wrote my letter of introduction. I had only just received my original Birth Certificate, and the emotional turmoil acknowledged as "reunion trauma" was just beginning.

## My Birthmother's Deepest, Darkest Secret

With the 1985 changes to their Adoption Laws, New Zealand has placed social workers strategically in all the major cities to facilitate the outpouring of reunions for adult adoptees and their birth parents.

I am living permanently in Australia, so I take advantage of the mediation by adoption social workers, to first locate my birth mother (in Palmerston North), and then to contact her.

I wrote a letter introducing myself, my husband, and my children. I enclose photos—and take a deep breath. Will she accept my presence in her life? Will she agree to a reunion? Or, as was her legal right, will she refuse?

I hold my breath. And wait. Haunted by the shadow of fear and the subconscious memory of abandonment at birth, anxiety and excitement wreak havoc within me. Not being used to the presence of such emotions, I will ultimately realize that my subconscious fear of another rejection fuels this chaos within me.

The letter from the social worker arrives first. She met with my birth mother. She would love to meet with me and my family, but my birth mother has asked me to wait six weeks whilst she visits her adult children (my brothers and sisters) to tell them I exist. In the forty years since my birth in Lower Hutt Maternity Ward, my birth mother has never told anyone of my existence. With the changing of the law in 1985, she had wondered where I might be. And, as the years drifted into 1988 and there was no message, no request for a reunion, the memory of our pregnancy and my birth was buried deep within her subconscious once again.

My birth mother was a high school teacher and counsellor. When she received a message from a local social worker for a private meeting in her home, she assumed it was about a student requiring support at her school.

My letter and photos had arrived at their destination.

D-Day. Beryl learns her daughter is alive and well and is requesting a reunion. How blessed am I to receive news that my birth mother wanted to meet with me, and my family. I am ecstatic and had the wisdom to be patient whilst she visits her adult children to reveal the deepest, darkest secret over her life. Her illegitimate baby, now forty-year-old daughter (their older sister) has asked to come home.

My birth mother visited first, flying into Sydney, giving us both time to get to know each other. Intimate strangers, the connection between us was an instant heart connection, because despite our painful birth experience, our mother/daughter bond was never severed. I was, fabulously, my birth mother replicated in heart, mind, and soul. Then my New Zealand brothers and sisters set down the welcome mat for myself, my husband and my children when we visited in 1991. The miracle of reunions had just begun.

## Our Sydney Reunion 28 December 1988

The happiest day of my life. I was working at Prince Henry Hospital, so George had collected my birth mother from Sydney Airport. Instead of driving her home he came to Prince Henry Hospital and parked outside my ground floor ward.

I happened to look out the ward window as my children jumped out of the car. And there was Mum climbing out the passenger side.

I was emotionally flooded—flooded with joy just at the sight of her standing there. I know I had a huge smile, as I said to my patients, "That's my mother out there." No-one knew the significance of that moment—I was meeting my birth mother for the first time. A breathtaking and beautiful moment simply seeing her standing outside next to the car.

My diary tells me how happy the family was that day. I commented on my husband's happiness, how blessed George felt getting to spend time with his new mother-in-law, as they drove from the airport. Even though he and I would later divorce, he and my birth mother would be friends for life.

Once again, the miraculous Hand of God over my life, restoring that which was lost.

## The Shoalhaven Adoption Support Group 1988 – 2000 Pain to Purpose Shared

When I realised New Zealand had led the way in changing their adoption laws, ahead of New South Wales, Australia (where I reside), I realised I wanted to bring the New Zealand change of adoption laws to NSW.

The Shoalhaven Adoption Support Group was the perfect platform for my birth mother and I to work together serving others.

We invited anyone affected by adoption laws to attend the meeting. Adult Adoptees. Birthparents. Adoptive Parents. With the closed adoption laws about to be changed, and reunions encouraged, this adoption support group was inclusive for all parties.

This was pioneering stuff. We were achieving something remarkable, and unheard of, when we invited anyone and everyone affected by the adoption laws to attend our meetings. We pioneered inclusiveness in our adoption community, and it was an outstanding success.

It was empowering to discover we needed each other to fully appreciate our own adoption pain and recognise the pain of others hurting in our community. We needed each other to fully appreciate our adoption issues regardless of where we were at in our adoption journey. We needed each other to heal, because healing will not take place when isolated and alone. Healing only takes place in relationships—meaningful relationships.

# Adoption is a Lifelong Journey

The primal wound. Genealogical bewilderment. Reunion trauma. Grief. None of these are unique to the adoption community. I learned that these are the consequences of infertility grief, baby loss, mother loss and father loss. They are, however, an integral part of my psychological and emotional health for life, impacting upon my values and beliefs, and my speech. Typical of those experiencing multiple layers of trauma and grief, my extroverted, storytelling brain can be rambling and digressive, frustrating for those waiting for me to get to the point of my story. I love how my daughter has solved this issue with an effective prompt. "Land that plane Mum. Land that plane."

I have come to realise that psychologically and emotionally I will never reach a state of "as if not adopted," this journey fluctuating in my subconscious like the incoming, and outgoing tides of the ocean. One moment I am courageous, strong and grounded in my identity, then the flow of sadness and grief insidiously emerges, causing me to withdraw from life and those around me. My healing time.

When God gifted me the presence of joy in my heart and soul in the midst of those snow-covered mountains surrounding Lake Coleridge, He provided me with a moment where I experienced myself as a joy filled child, whole and complete. Surely a miracle for a ten-year-old child. I embraced a core value that life, on the other side of nausea and throwing up, could be an extraordinary adventure waiting to be lived and shared. This value is the fabulous dictator over my life.

My greatest adventures involved embracing my multiple families and heritage. I am adopted-and-Maori, and proud to be embracing (and be embraced by), empowering and healing relationships and connections. Not just some of them. All of them. Deceased family, and present family. Every reunion is a miracle. Life is a miracle.

I experience life with deep gratitude. I treasure my loving children, the families who have welcomed me with open arms, and the friends and companions who have shared my journey. My story is a testament to restoration, adventure, and God's grace.

*Praise God who orchestrated and planned my life.*
*Praise God for every experience and every adventure.*
*Praise God for every person, past and present, He*
*has brought into my life.*
*Praise God for the Spirit of Adventure and the*
*Miracle of Life.*

## ShonaRobyn Eisenberg

SR Restoration Life Coach

# ABOUT THE AUTHOR

ShonaRobyn is a mum, nana, daughter, sister, and aunty, with deep connections to multiple families—a reflection of her journey as an adopted, Māori-born woman. She is a nurse, educator, life coach, and a passionate adventurer who has embraced life's diverse paths. Now living in Australia, ShonaRobyn proudly celebrates her New Zealand roots and Māori heritage, holding fast to the belief that every person, every story, and every adventure matters.

Her childhood, spent among the breathtaking landscapes of New Zealand, instilled in her a profound love for the outdoors. This connection to nature has always brought beauty, awe, and healing into her life. ShonaRobyn's adventurous spirit led her on journeys around the world—riding motorbikes across continents and walking the Camino—experiences that shaped her character and deepened her love for exploration. These adventures became a path of celebration, marking significant moments in her life and guiding her toward personal growth and self-discovery.

For ShonaRobyn, adventure is more than a thrill—it is a journey of restoration. As she navigated the complexities of her adoptive and biological families, she found healing and peace in the vast panoramas of the world, with the landscapes mirroring the ups and downs of her life. Through these journeys, she uncovered deeper truths about her identity and relationships, finding renewal and clarity along the way.

**Find Me:**

Facebook: www.facebook.com/shonarobyn.eisenberg

Email: sreisenberg48@gmail.com

# COURAGEOUS VOICES UNLOCKED

*If there was one thing I learned through my journey to finding my birth mother and developing a relationship with her, it's how to speak up for your needs. The next co-author,* **DeAnne***, shares the same tenacity and boldness needed to speak out against the injustices of this world, including the ones that try to fly under the radar in our current society.*

# DEDICATION

This is for every woman who has ever felt unseen, unheard, or unworthy of the dreams God has placed in her heart.

Remember, you are fearfully and wonderfully made, crafted with purpose by the hands of the Creator. God's love for you is boundless, and He calls you to stand tall, walk in His truth, and reign as the Queen He designed you to be.

May this journey bring you great healing, so that you may in turn heal others with the love and grace you've received. Embrace His love, unlock the treasures within you, and boldly pursue the path He has set before you. You are cherished, powerful, and destined to shine in the fullness of your divine purpose.

M. DeAnne Morrell

# RIDE THE WAVE OF COURAGE
## EMBRACE YOUR DESTINY


## M. DeAnne Morrell

Founder, Owner, Divine Anointed Woman Academy

### New Brunswick, Canada


*"Courage is an essential virtue that empowers us to face our fears, overcome obstacles, and pursue our true calling with unwavering determination."*
~M. DeAnne Morrell

## Embracing Courage Beyond Comfort

Embracing courage means stepping out of our comfort zones, finding our own voice, and standing firm in our beliefs and values. It is through courage that we discover our strengths, define our paths, and shape our destinies. In the following stories, I will share a few of (but not all) my personal encounters with courage, illustrating how embracing this powerful force has guided me toward fulfilling my destiny. These experiences highlight the transformative impact of courage, inspiring us to live authentically and pursue our divine purposes with confidence and resilience.

## Dare to Dream, Dare to Do

It was a sweltering summer afternoon on the blueberry farm, the kind of day where the sun beat down relentlessly and the air was heavy with the sweet scent of ripe blueberries.

I had worked tirelessly for hours, my hands stained with purple juice. I had collected 17 flats by mid-day, a personal best, and was eager to call it a day. At just 13 years old, I landed this job on the farm, and it was my first taste of real employment.

Suddenly, the sound of a motorcycle echoed through the air, growing louder with each passing second. Pete, my co-worker, looked up from his own picking and squinted into the distance.

"Who's coming down here on a motorcycle?" he asked, his voice raised above the din of the engine.

I followed his gaze and spotted a black Harley-Davidson churning up dust as it made its way down the dirt path. My heart skipped a beat as I realized who it was—my dad! He was riding into the farm on his trusty bike, and he'd come to take me home.

I felt a rush of excitement as I waved eagerly at him. Pete grinned and nodded in approval. "That's your dad?" Pete asked. "He's quite the cool guy!" he said. "He sure is!" I exclaimed! "My dad is the coolest because he's always taking me on amazing adventures. He's so brave and adventurous! When we go exploring in the woods or climb mountains together, he shows me the most exciting things—like how to build a campfire and spot animals in their natural homes. I love how he's not afraid to try new things and teaches me to be brave too. He took me on my first roller coaster ride, airplane ride and now motorcycle ride! He's my hero!" I shouted enthusiastically!

My dad pulled up alongside us, kicking up clouds of dirt as he came to a stop. "Hi there! Ready to head out?" he asked. I was on top of the world.

I nodded enthusiastically, already climbing onto the back of the bike behind him. He handed me a helmet and helped me strap it on before settling in himself. As we pulled out of the farm and onto the highway, I felt alive—the wind in my hair, the sun on my face, and clinging to my dad's waist.

I loved watching him navigate the roads. He'd point out interesting landmarks and tell stories about his own adventures on the bike.

"Watch, DeAnne," he'd say, nodding towards an approaching biker. "I'll wave at him, and he'll wave back." And sure enough, wave they did! It was our special tradition—bonding over our shared love of motorcycles.

As we rode off into the distance, I felt grateful for this chance to share another experience with my dad. The wind whipping through my hair, I knew that this was what being alive felt like—free, exhilarating, and full of adventure.

## Paving My Way Forward

As I grew older, my desire to ride on the back of a motorcycle never faded. In fact, it only intensified. I spent many years being a passenger on the back of friends' bikes, enjoying the wind in my hair and the freedom that came with it. But deep down, I knew I wanted more. I yearned to be the one in control, to feel the power and responsibility of piloting my own bike.

One summer, while in LA, I stumbled upon a striking woman with long, flowing black hair that cascaded down her back like a waterfall. She emerged from a store and straddled a Fatboy Harley-Davidson, revving the engine before riding off into the distance. I watched in awe as she disappeared into the traffic, feeling a spark ignite within me. That's what I wanted—to ride with confidence and style.

Years went by, and my dream finally became a reality in my 30s. I decided to take the plunge and buy my own bike. My ultimate goal was to ride the 83 Shovelhead in my dad's garage, which had always fascinated me. However, as I began taking motorcycle safety courses and working towards my license, reality set in. The 83 Shovelhead was a beast of a bike, weighing nearly 500 pounds.

But as I gained confidence on the smaller bike the course provided, I began to feel anxious about shifting to the heavier Shovelhead. During safety course sessions, I found myself struggling to come to a stop smoothly, especially on inclines. Unlike cars, where you can turn into a turn while stopped, motorcycles require you to keep the wheel straight when stopping on an angle. Any deviation would send you tumbling to the ground—exactly what happened during one particularly grueling session.

I recall one day during class when I was determined to master the art of stopping on a hill. As we approached a gentle incline, my instructor shouted "Stop!" just as I was gaining speed. I downshifted and attempted to bring the bike to a halt, but my lack of experience betrayed me. The bike leaned precariously to one side, and before I knew it, we were both sliding across the pavement.

My instructor helped me up, laughing reassuringly. "It's okay, DeAnne! You're not alone! We all go down sometimes." But deep down, I was mortified. Had I really been foolish enough to think I could handle something as powerful as the Shovelhead? The fear crept in like a slow-moving fog, casting doubt over my dreams of riding that majestic machine.

Yet, as I sat on that pavement, nursing my scraped knee and bruised ego, something inside me refused to give up. Maybe it was my dad's words echoing in my mind— "You can do this!" Maybe it was the memory of that striking woman on her Fatboy Harley-Davidson—whoever she was—or maybe it was simply the thrill of being alive.

I looked up at my instructor and smiled sheepishly. "You know what? I think I need some more practice."

## Fear to Fearless

At the time, I was married to Avery, and we had just visited a motorcycle dealer together. I had been itching to get my own bike, and the Honda 250 Rebel caught my eye. But Avery and the dealer convinced me that I would tire of its smaller size and want something bigger in just a month. They suggested I opt for the 650 Shadow instead—a whopping 500 pounds of machine.

I hesitated, but with their assurance that it was the right choice, I reluctantly agreed. Little did I know, that decision would haunt me for years to come.

One fateful day, Avery and I decided to go for a ride— him in front, me behind. We came to a stop on a hill, and as I shifted my weight slightly to the right, the bike tipped over. Avery quickly jumped off his bike to help me upright mine, and as we struggled to get it back on its wheels, I felt a sense of dread wash over me. This wasn't fun anymore. I wouldn't be able to ride solo without someone there to help me every step of the way.

The more we rode together, the more I grew anxious about being dependent on Avery's assistance. Eventually, I started hating what was once my passion—the freedom and thrill of riding. The 650 Shadow sat idle in our garage for months before I finally sold it.

But even as I let go of my beloved bike, my love for riding never faded. It was like an ember burning deep within me, waiting to be reignited. One day, I made the bold decision to return to my roots and get that little Honda 250 Rebel. It didn't matter if it was smaller; it was perfect for me.

As I started riding again, just a few miles at a time, I began to rebuild my confidence. The Rebel proved to be an excellent teacher, gentle yet firm in its instruction. With each passing day, I grew more comfortable on it, learning to navigate turns and hills with ease.

Eventually, I felt ready for a bigger adventure. So, with just a backpack, tent, and my trusty Rebel by my side, I embarked on a two-week journey that spanned over 1,000 miles. The wind in my hair, the sun on my face, and the roar of the engine beneath me—it was exhilarating! I would have missed out on this incredible experience had I let fear and doubt dictate my path.

My story is a reminder that everyone learns at their own pace. We shouldn't compare ourselves to others or expect others to fit into our mold. We must allow people to grow and learn at their own speed—whether it's on two wheels or in life itself.

## Awaken Your Best Self

As I gaze out at the vast expanse of the ocean, my mind wanders to the one place I've yet to explore: the Great Barrier Reef in Australia. The thought of descending into that underwater world, teeming with life and mystery, sends shivers down my spine. For me, being underwater is like entering an alternate universe—a realm where we can't survive, and its inhabitants can't thrive in our world. I'm drawn to this alien landscape, fascinated by the wonders that lurk beneath the surface.

My journey to becoming a scuba diver began in an Olympic-sized swimming pool in the shallow end. I was determined to master the art of mask clearing, but it eluded me. No matter how hard I tried, I just couldn't seem to get it right. Meanwhile, my fellow students were already learning life-saving techniques in the deep end. My instructor recognized my frustration and took the time to work with me one-on-one. It took a little extra effort, but soon I was joining the group in the deep end, learning how to provide oxygen to my buddy in case of an emergency.

I excelled at this new skill, and it seemed that when it came down to saving someone's life, I had a natural talent for it. It was okay that mask clearing took a little longer; I just needed to grow at my own pace and be allowed to nurture what needed nurturing.

Wreck Diving in Dutch Springs Quarry
Bethlehem, Pennsylvania 2015

As I grew older and wiser, I realized that this experience had taught me a valuable lesson. We often need mentors who can guide us at our own pace, helping us stay motivated and encouraged as we work towards our goals. This doesn't mean we should become complacent or procrastinate; rather, it means we should seek a pace that allows us to excel without feeling overwhelmed.

This understanding has helped me approach other areas of my life, including my passion for riding motorcycles. After a disappointing experience with a heavy bike, I almost gave up on my dream of riding solo. But I didn't let fear and doubt win; instead, I took the time to learn at my own pace and eventually found the perfect bike for me.

As I reflect on my journey, I'm reminded of the importance of knowing oneself. Taking deep dives into our fundamental core can help us understand our strengths and weaknesses, embracing the good and challenging the bad. Dreams aren't meant to die or go unfulfilled; they're meant to be lived.

So, don't bury your dreams—live them. Take the time to learn at your own pace, and don't be afraid to ask for help when you need it. With patience, persistence, and a willingness to learn from our mistakes, we can overcome any obstacle and turn our dreams into reality.

## The Quest for Self-Knowledge

I recently delved into the world of a popular personality test, and I discovered that I possess an iD style, characterized by a unique blend of charisma, assertiveness, and results-driven determination. With an Influence-Dominance score, I've found that I'm naturally drawn to building strong relationships, connecting with others effortlessly, and driving decisions to achieve my goals.

But what does this mean for me? Understanding my personality has allowed me to recognize my strengths and areas for improvement. It's empowered me to adapt to different situations with ease, knowing that my natural tendencies are influencing my thoughts and actions.

Moreover, this self-awareness has given me a newfound appreciation for the diversity of human personalities. When faced with disagreements or misunderstandings, I've come to realize that it's not about being right or wrong—it's simply a matter of different perspectives and preferences. Imagine if more people took the time to understand their fundamental selves and those around them. The world would be filled with greater empathy, understanding, and unity.

I've seen this play out in my own relationships. When I'm with someone who has a different personality type, I've noticed that we often struggle to understand each other. But by taking the time to learn about each other's styles and tendencies, we can bridge the gap and find common ground. This deeper understanding facilitates stronger connections, greater harmony, and a deeper sense of love.

I believe that this is the key to breaking down barriers and building more meaningful relationships. By embracing our unique personalities and acknowledging the differences that make us human, we can create a world where love and understanding thrive. So, take the time to discover your fundamental self—you never know the profound impact it could have on your life and those around you.

## Stepping into Sacred Powers

I strongly believe that it's crucial to boldly petition Father God in Heaven to ignite the extraordinary gifts of the Holy Spirit within us, granting us the power of revelation, discernment, wisdom, and knowledge. This divine empowerment is essential for women to stand confidently in their God-given identity and fulfill their divine purpose.

Unfortunately, many women are often held back by the suffocating grip of patriarchy, a system where men wield power and authority over women. This insidious system has far-reaching and devastating consequences, perpetuating a culture of male dominance and female subjugation. Women are frequently expected to assume secondary roles and prioritize the needs of others before their own, leading to limited access to education, employment, and economic opportunities. Moreover, it promotes a culture of gender-based violence and discrimination, restricting women's autonomy and decision-making power.

Patriarchy also perpetuates harmful gender stereotypes, portraying women as inferior or less capable than men. This can lead to internalized oppression and self-doubt, causing women to question their worth and abilities. Furthermore, it can stifle their creativity, innovation, and contributions to society, preventing them from reaching their full potential.

It's essential to recognize that patriarchy is a deeply ingrained system that requires a profound shift in societal values and power dynamics to achieve true gender equality and social justice. Only through a concerted effort can we dismantle this oppressive system and create a world where women are valued, respected, and empowered to thrive in their God-given roles. By seeking the empowerment of the Holy Spirit, we can break free from the shackles of patriarchy and live as the divine daughters of God we were created to be.

## Exposing Stealth Oppression

I experienced a traumatic ordeal at a church that, despite its outward appearance of being Christian, was actually infected with the toxic teachings of Puritan legalism. As I navigated this challenging period, marked by both professional success and personal growth, I struggled to understand why I was facing such intense trials. In my moments of desperation, I would pour out my heart to God in prayer, seeking answers. His response was always the same: "I need you to expose them."

At the time, I was unclear about who "they" referred to, but as my journey unfolded, I began to realize that it was the very church I had trusted that was causing harm. Despite their outward display of love and devotion to Jesus, they were secretly holding me in a negative light, condemning my past and controlling my present with elements of witchcraft through the oath I had taken with them. Once the Holy Spirit gave me the discernment and revelation that it was the church, I was able to renounce and denounce them in the mighty name of Jesus and place His blood on that oath I took. God did not want me in a church that was abusing me. The sad thing is, I could tell other women were suffering in this church too. When I denounced them, my life got better.

This experience was not unique to me; many women have faced similar exploitation and manipulation at the hands of patriarchal systems. It's crucial to recognize that these institutions often masquerade as Christian, but their true intent is to maintain power and control over women's lives.

In my journey of healing and growth, I came to understand the importance of awakening to the supernatural powers of the Holy Spirit. Through this revelation, I gained insight into the machinations of those who seek to harm others and began to see the truth behind their actions.

It's essential for women to recognize that they are not alone in this struggle. Many have been silenced or shamed by patriarchal systems, but it's time to break free from the shackles of oppression. By embracing our supernatural identity and walking in the power of the Holy Spirit, we can overcome the forces that seek to hold us back.

In my story, I saw how a church that claimed to love me was actually working against me, trying to humiliate me so that no one would listen. But Jesus is the one who truly loves us, and He calls us to lead and serve with Him. Let us trust His voice above all else and reject the oppressive systems that seek to silence and dominate us.

## Claim Your Divine Authority

To rise above the challenges and overcome the forces of oppression, you must be bold, fearless, and unwavering in your trust in the Lord. Embrace the supernatural gifts of the Holy Spirit and allow Him to guide and protect you as you navigate the treacherous waters of life. Keep your eyes fixed on Jesus, and let the Holy Spirit lift you up to walk on the water of His divine authority.

Don't let the world's oppressive systems hold you back from achieving your destiny. Instead, receive the gifts of the Holy Spirit and take your rightful place as a leader, equal and respected alongside men. Remember, God's Word declares that a woman is not governed by a man, but rather respected, heard, cherished, and loved as Christ loves us.

Make no mistake: God was not pleased with the patriarchal systems that sought to oppress me, His anointed vessel. He called me to lead, and He calls you too. You are His beloved child, empowered by His divine love and strength.

So, don't let fear hold you back from pursuing your dreams. Embrace your destiny, conquer your doubts, and trust in the divine power of the Holy Spirit within you to lead you to fulfillment and purpose. Rise up, take your mountain, and shine brightly in the light of God's love. You are a daughter of the Most High God and He needs you to fulfill your unique purpose on this earth. Beyond this obedience and calling that God has placed on your life, there are others eagerly awaiting your impact.

> "You do not need to know precisely what is
> happening, or exactly where it is all going. What you
> need is to recognize the possibilities and challenges

offered by the present moment, and to embrace
them with courage, faith, and hope."
~ Thomas Merton, *Conversations with Thomas Merton*

*M. De Anne Morrell*

Founder/Owner/CEO
Divine Anointed Woman Academy
MD Morrell Voice/Verse Academy
Nocturnal Red Music Media Group
Mammal Babies Boutique

I chose to write a poem inspired by the title of this book because "Courageous Voices Unlocked" speaks volumes about how we are called to embrace our lives with boldness and courage. It resonated with me deeply, and I felt compelled to pay homage to its powerful message. Through this poem, I honor the essence of the book—capturing the spirit of courage, vulnerability, and authenticity. You'll find my poem only within these pages, as a testament to the transformative impact this book has had on me. On the next page, my words echo its message.

## Courageous Voices Unlocked

Courage may be a resounding gong but is more often the quiet
    grace
Of showing up with heart upright and steadfast in your space
Unified steps into the dawn when shadows loom and crowd
Rise from the stillness of the morn let courage speak aloud
Alignment lies in daily grinds of every tireless try
Growing pathways of feathered dreams lit with hope on high
Eminent courage breathes whispered tones "You've weathered
    dark's embrace"
Omnipotent in fierce fiery trials courage always holds its place
Unmask your authentic soul and let your voice fly free
Show bold acts of creation and unveil your destiny

Vulnerability though tender carries the weight of gold
Open its gentle essence so your saga brave unfolds
It's not the roaring triumphs but the courage to be seen
Celebrating your voice and power sharpening your every dream
Embark on challenges ahead as they sculpt your inner might
Step out on planks of faith and bring the dawn from darkest night

Uniquely touch the world with gifts that only you can bring
Narrate your story of healing and make the silent sing
Looking forward on your journey let your heart lead the way
Optimistic in a world hungry for your truth on display
Create room for quiet valor and let your spirit shine bright
Keen acts of courage transforms the darkness to white light
Embrace within your core affirming "I am brave, I am true"
Dear courage as your guiding star there's nothing you can't do

# ABOUT THE AUTHOR

M. DeAnne Morrell is the founder and owner of Divine Anointed Woman Academy, Nocturnal Red Music Media Group, and Mammal Babies Boutique. A certified life coach with an Associate's in Biblical Studies and a Bachelor's in Business and Ministry, she is currently pursuing a Master of Arts in Business and Ministry. Known affectionately by her students as "Coach MD" she is also an award-winning multi-instrumentalist, singer, songwriter, keynote speaker, recording artist, voice actor, three times #1 Amazon international bestselling author, music publisher, and award-winning entrepreneur. With numerous Billboard Achievement Awards and other accolades, DeAnne has spent over half her life captivating audiences, performing more than 200 times annually for two decades. An active voting member of the Recording Academy (the Grammys) for over 20 years, she has been featured on radio, TV, and online forums. When not speaking or performing on stage, DeAnne empowers women to ignite the supernatural power of the Holy Spirit within, guides musicians in crafting and monetizing their unique sound, and creates bespoke poetry art through her work at Mammal Babies.

**Find Me:**

Facebook:
www.facebook.com/coach.md.morrell
www.facebook.com/divineanointedwoman.academy
www.facebook.com/mammalbabiesboutique

Website:
www.mdmorrell.com/

www.divineanointedwoman.academy/
https://mammalbabiesboutique.ca/

<u>YouTube</u>:
www.youtube.com/@mdmorrellvoiceverseacademy
www.youtube.com/@nocturnalredmusic

<u>Email</u>:
coach@mdmorrell.com
info@divineanointedwoman.academy

<u>Schedule a Call</u>: https://calendly.com/coachmdmorrell

<u>Free Gift</u>:
www.mdmorrell.com/free-gift
www.divineanointedwoman.academy/free-gift

# COURAGEOUS VOICES UNLOCKED

*There was no one I was going to let tell me who I was or who I have been created to be—except God. My purpose is my purpose, unique to me and what God has predestined for me.* **Nic,** *the next co-author, shares her journey to becoming purpose-driven and kingdom-minded as well in her chapter, "Beauty for Ashes."*

# DEDICATION

My Chapter is dedicated to my three amazing children Brooke, Jack, and Ashton, to my mentor and soul sister Lorraine Gale, to those that knew God had more for me to unlock before I did and called me higher, to those that have been part of my journey to date, and to you, the reader. May you be reminded and encouraged that wherever you find yourself along your journey, it isn't as it seems. God still has so much to unlock in your world.

The best is still yet to come.
Nic xo

# BEAUTY FOR ASHES
## SURVIVING TO THRIVING

## Nic Henry Jones

Author, Entrepreneur, Business Thought Leader and
Strategist, Digital Marketer. Changemaker

**Bridgewater, Adelaide Hills, South Australia**

*"We've been given everything we need to live,
thrive and be whole human beings. It's up to us
to use what we've been given and pursue
the complete unlocking of it."*
~ Nic Henry Jones

## Introduction

I knew from the age of twelve, I was going to be on a different path, my understanding of 'normal' was not something I wanted to live. In my teenage years I had the world at my feet. I had a clear understanding of my identity, my future, and an awareness of the change I knew I needed to initiate on a number of levels. But as with many of us, this was all thrown into confusion with multiple life situations and major setbacks, requiring me to give up the very life I had such a clear vision for. Finding myself very lost, confused, wanting to opt out of life completely, walking through 15 tough years of heartbreak, illness, doubt, confusion, deep emotional pain, and even walking away from faith in God. Years later, I found myself picking up the paintbrush in my hand and allowing God to reveal the Masterpiece He didn't give up on, and watching Him rebuild me, bit by bit, as he took me from surviving to thriving, to then taking me to a place of helping others do the same.

## Life to Ruins, Then Back to Life

I grew up in Central Queensland in a Christian home. As a family we were always at church multiple times a day, as my parents were both in leadership roles at different times. I was always a few years ahead of others my age. I was a Sunday School teacher at twelve, writing lesson plans and being part of a team. I wanted to be a teacher when I grew up. By fifteen, I was a youth leader, and as a team we ran Teen Challenge Programs for the youth of our town on top of our usual church youth activities. From the age of twelve, I was also on the worship team, by sixteen I was worship leading, seventeen, worship leading from the keyboard, and by eighteen, all I wanted to do was head off to Bible College.

As a teenager, I was truly invested in something higher than myself. Alongside Church commitments, I worked casual jobs, home-schooling myself Grade 11 and 12 (by choice), and on Youth Committee's with our local Council. Unlike other teenagers, all I wanted to do was serve God and honor the things he had put inside of me. I had zero desire to attend University or travel the world. I only wanted to be in ministry and be engaged in something deeper and higher, because 'people' seemed to really matter to me, more than normal. These formative years have become incredibly important to how I run my race and manage multiple projects and contexts, in my unique lane today.

I got married young, and we decided to leave Queensland and attend the Bible College of South Australia (BCSA) together with the intention of going into Full-time Ministry. I was the only Pentecostal there as it was a multidenominational College, which I wanted to embrace on purpose. I wanted to understand Theology and the truth behind denominations seemingly being at war with each other in the late 1990's. My brain had this God-given capacity to question and challenge things in ways most people didn't or couldn't (absolutely crucial to what he puts in front of me now, as this is my lane). I was honored to be Student President for 2 out of my 3 years there, and we were offered my dream role as Youth Pastors in regional South Australia with an incredible couple who were also Queenslanders. But my house wasn't in order, so I had to decline the invitation, and stand down from the very life I felt I was called to. I started grieving the loss (perceived) of the life I envisaged and had positioned for. Nothing made sense or looked like the life I thought God had for me, and it was a far cry from the life I thought I would be living. After growing up surrounded by people, I was stuck in another state of Australia, alone.

I became very unwell with a lung condition called Sarcoidiosis. In 2010, I landed in hospital for a week at 51kgs with a relapse of this condition, Pneumonia and another infection. I could not breathe, I was completely spent in every way, and not wanting to live anymore. At this point I had no direction, or confirmation I was even on a path. I was angry at God and those around me. Not long after I had a marriage breakdown, and with 3 young kids (6 and 3 yr old twins) in the mix, it was really tough.

I completely walked away from God. I thought, if this is all God has for me, there's no point continuing in faith. Why would I bother getting out of bed on a Sunday, spending time praying or worshipping, because it only had me land in a place of pain and confusion—especially confused because my intentions were always pure towards God and his plans for me. Maybe I had made wrong choices and because of that, I've missed the boat. All I knew was I was at rock bottom.

During this period of illness and uncertainty around my future, I did something quite radical—I started a marketing company. I had run a few hobby businesses and saw how they were gaining traction on social media, and I also saw brands doing a pretty poor job of platforms such as Facebook, and so I saw a need, and provided a solution. I was creative, passionate about helping others, and seemed to be a few steps ahead mindset wise of those in business. I saw marketing as a way of honoring my passions including training and unlocking things in people, and I thought if I'm not going into ministry, I may as well go into business! I was totally unqualified (I attended Bible College not University), yet God was on it and to this day this business is still my primary source of income, and also the platform from which a lot of my other initiatives stem from, including the incredible opportunities God gives me to work with various ministries and charities. My business was all I had to hold onto in those early stages, and it's been my one constant, next to God.

## He's Always Working All Things Together for Our Good

God doesn't wait for your life to be in order, before He positions you. Quite often God will position you whilst you are in your pain, so you are always moving towards your next few steps and be ready to function powerfully, or already be functioning, when God turns the pain into gain. It's not a 'then' and 'now' in God, He's always working all things together for our good, at every step. He's threading silver linings and gold threads in your life journey throughout every season, situation, win or loss.

For the first few years of my business journey, all I could do was be faithful with every step, regardless how seemingly small, try to survive day by day, and hope for better days ahead. My emotional and physical state was not good, yet I had to find the energy to be strong, to look like I was somewhat successful so people would use my services. I knew I had to push through. You know those seasons where all you can do is make sure your inbox is cleared, the kids are fed, and the dishes are done? Where you hope and pray, with no faith, that this isn't actually the end? It was soul destroying and very difficult. I contemplated suicide many times, because I felt there was no purpose left for me here.

And while I managed to regroup in some ways, building up my business to a certain level, finding new norms in life and pushing to create new ones, and gaining some kind of stability, another heartbreak, more tough situations and seasons later, along with the challenges of being a single parent, I had my second rock bottom experience (both within 4 years). It was a period of really having to push hard to make things happen, all while being very aware that my existence was not a strong grounded one. And while I don't generally roll like this, it was a 'fake it till you make it' type of season. It was pure faith, with no evidence.

At this point all I knew was that I couldn't get any lower, and the only way out was up. My identity was completely smashed into pieces, and I did not know who I was. For the first time in my life, I had major anxiety where I couldn't even leave the home at times. Being around people was too overwhelming for me and depression became my norm. I was seeing Naturopaths, Counsellors, Psychologists, you name it, I needed help and answers, immediately.

## God Will Do His Bit: When We Do Ours

I remember my counsellor asking me if I was doing any self-care. I pretty much asked her what that was because I had spent so many years helping everyone else and wasn't taking any time for me! I was relying on other people to help care for me, but I quickly realised, there wasn't anyone else, it was up to me, being led into alignment by God. I had it the wrong way around. I realised I had no chance of getting out of my survival mode and thriving until I started to get some alignment, so I was able to function out of a place of wholeness, or a degree of. I had to pursue wholeness not perfection, it was all about perspective. The decisions you make in your 'survive,' are very different to the decisions you make in your 'thrive,' even in a partial thrive.

> *"Wholeness is not a destination, it's a state of being.*
> *It's something we partner with God on, and to position for*
> *every day of our lives. And different seasons will require a*
> *different version of you. Wholeness is alignment to*
> *and unity with your true Identity in Christ."*

I could never understand growing up how people could walk away from God, yet I did it not because I wanted to, because I was stuck in hope deferred, and now I understand. I landed back in church in 2016 after four years of trying to do it on my own. I didn't want to be there, it was confronting and scary at the same time, though I knew that it was an act of obedience to God, and it was absolutely the doorway to the life I was called to live, it was my only way up. I found a beautiful community of people I hadn't had since I left Queensland thirteen years earlier and recommitted my life to God. I remember driving up and down the Freeway that I lived close to, with the song 'Ruins' by Hillsong playing over and over and over, with tears streaming down my face. I just wanted God to bring the ruins to life. If I was still breathing, He must have not given up on me yet, so I shouldn't give up on me either.

> *"If you give up on God, you actually give up on yourself. Your*
> *true Identity can only be found in Him. It's up to us to partner*

*with him to work through, unpack and unlock this."*

Over a period of eighteen months, He changed everything. It was very incremental at first, but it started to snowball as the months went on. Making very intentional decisions, and with my biggest alignment back to God in place, I was able to start moving in the right direction, gaining confidence along the way. We never ever have to start from scratch in God. He never gives up on us. He turns our pain into gain and our mourning into joy, but sometimes that requires lots of surrender, prayer and worship.

He started to open doors I didn't see coming. I started to feel alive again, like I could physically breathe. My life turned a complete 180 degrees on every level, and I was a completely different person. My business income doubled and I had some big corporate clients, my health ended up resolving to a level I didn't think it would, I felt free-er than ever before, I found my tribe, and as I was doing the best I ever had financially through my business, I bought my dream car and upleveled my world with my dream style of furniture, and all matching too! I was excited about the future again and what God would have for me.

If it meant that by 45, I had been forced to carve out a new path to re-align with what God had for me, take the time to work out who I really was in Him before the pain of life kicked in, and what my purpose was, then I was blessed to walk into the second half of my life, with clarity, confidence, purpose, passion, and direction. I was one blessed woman, and a woman on a serious mission. Not everyone pushes through to be able to experience and see that for themselves. We look to external things to fill the void, instead of going within and addressing the void, with alignment back to our creator, and our true Identity.

*"There are some things in God you don't get to experience unless you have walked through some significant fire."*

## Be Faithful with What is in Front of You

There were a few things that really stood out to me as big lessons or strategies while I was regrouping. I learnt the concept of 'being faithful with what was in front of me.' We hear about being faithful with big things a lot, but every little step mattered in those crucial moments, and every decision still matters. I used to walk into Church, expecting and believing that every time I turned up in obedience, God would heal me just that bit more. I knew I couldn't turn my life around overnight, but I knew I could be faithful with what God had put in front of me, like stepping stones are placed for movement, direction and safety. And then when I was much stronger, I aimed to do 10% better every year, spiritually, physically, mentally, emotionally. I wanted to run the race with grit, grace and purpose, in His strength, under his anointing.

*"I wanted my feet to hit the ground every morning with one prayer on my heart, that God would 'order my steps, and lead with favor.' I still pray this prayer today."*

## Intention & Alignment

As I was processing my journey, I remember the day in 2018 that God spoke to me very clearly, about 'intention' and 'alignment.' I had a deep feeling those two words were powerful and were going to frame my future. God showed me one day that my life was in fact a Masterpiece. The outline for my world was spoken into being BEFORE I was even born. I was created on purpose, for purpose. But I still had a choice to live by default (in our broken state of humanity) or choose to walk and live with intention. I chose to embrace intention. I didn't want to settle for anything less than God's best for me, and it would take a lifetime to unlock and experience it all.

*"Before I formed you in the womb I knew you; Before you were born I sanctified you; I ordained you a prophet to the nations"*
(Jeremiah 1:5 NKJV).

I had the paintbrush in my hand, with the paints nearby, I had everything I needed to thrive and live a beautiful life that would honor God, unlock my potential and my best life. I had the chance to find and create joy and fulfilment, coloring up my world with all of my favourite things, to be able to truly authentically 'thrive.' He knew. He knew the why, what, when, and how. Nothing surprised Him. I couldn't thwart or change the plans He had for me. I just had the chance to live some significant pain to be able to walk in authority in helping others on their journey, all while initiating change in the future. My life wasn't over, it was just starting. I watched Him turn my pain into gain, and I knew He would do that for others too.

## Seeking a Word from God for Each Year

One day, out of nowhere, I asked God to give me a 'word' for my year. When it seems like so much needs to be different, it can be overwhelming, but one 'word' gives you something to focus on, it gives your mind, body, soul and spirit some direction on what to pursue and ways change can be initiated. Some of my words have been 're-calibration, thrive, ease, and breakthrough. This year, my word was 'build.' I knew that there was a special anointing on this year to build business, write my next book, and begin to get prepared for the second half of my life. It's amazing what happens when your brain starts to look for the very things that align with that word, and how God fast tracks things when we pursue alignment with what he is already planning on doing in our lives.

## Beauty for Ashes

Fast forward to 2024, I am not even the same person I was 20 years ago. I look younger today than I did 10, 15, and 20 years ago, and I have never been healthier. I live a beautiful life surrounded by the most incredible people, in one of the most beautiful parts of Australia. I am clear on my Identity and who I am in Christ, living out my purpose and passions quite effortlessly in everything I do across multiple contexts. I get to be a teacher for adults, guiding, challenging, championing and empowering them in business and life, calling them higher.

God continues to put me in very unconventional places and spaces, doing very unconventional things in unconventional ways. I don't have any qualifications outside of my Bible College Certificate, yet God taps into my purpose and the things He has gifted me with. I am an unqualified digital marketer, Business & Life Coach, and lover of all things 'change,' but he has gifted me many opportunities to initiate change and unlock potential. I get to write books based on my experience, what I know of God and what he continues to reveal, not my qualifications, and I also find myself in industry, business and ministry contexts with the opportunity to speak life, give strategy, and help them unlock their potential. My businesses are my mission field and an outworking of my purpose. I'm not limited by educational certificates, denominations, frameworks (some of which aren't working), or other people's limitations. God leads and guides me every step of the way.

## God Wastes Nothing

Perfect life? No, but I am living proof that God can bring beauty from ashes. He just threads those gold and silver linings throughout your story, and each year builds on the previous if we are faithful with it. He wants to turn your pain into gain, graves into gardens, and usher in joy in the morning, along with new mercies every single day. I look around my home at night, when everything has been said and done, surrounded by beautiful things that speak to me, with a deep contentment, 24/7 conversation with God, and so much gratitude.

God wastes nothing, He is so faithful. He works all things together for our good in the most powerful of ways, that we can only see in hindsight. We're not a product of the past, we're a product of the Cross. God isn't surprised by the bit 'in the middle,' or the tension between what was and what will be.

Have you had to give up, or are you grieving the 'life you thought you were going to live'? My prayer is you will know that God isn't done with you yet.

Keep walking! Stay expectant. And remember if you woke up with air in your lungs, he hasn't given up on you, so you shouldn't give up either. And until it's your time to go to glory for eternity, we have a life to live, impact and influence to have, and a legacy to be built for the next Generation.

If you worked on identity, alignment and intention for the next 12 months, could you start to be where you've always wanted to be? Working on alignment for 6 months, will have you 5 years ahead of the 'normal' you.

So, what are you waiting for?

# ABOUT THE AUTHOR

Nic Henry Jones is a purpose-driven creative visionary, Entrepreneur, Business Strategist and Thought Leader, Coach, Educator, two-time Author of 'The Christian Entrepreneur' and 'Your Life Your Masterpiece,' and Changemaker at Hackable. Nic is highly passionate about people, purpose, business, change, and community and not only runs businesses. She is the General Manager of the Deborah Business Education Hub including The Deborah Conference, and supports the team and serves on the Board of the Agape Star Christian School in Uganda. In her spare time, she loves to create cheese platters and grazing boards at The Platter Co Australia.

**Find Me:**

Facebook: www.facebook.com/NicHenryJones

Find her Books: https://yourlifeyourmasterpiece.com/

Sign up for updates on new Book: https://hackable.au/

Email: hello@hackable.au

Schedule a Call: http://calendly.com/marketmemarketing

# Courageous Voices Unlocked

*Honestly, everything I went through, my struggles and my trials made me who I am today. It took me a little while to learn how to keep my eyes focused on things from above, but once I did, it completely changed how I live out my calling. The next co-author, **Cynthia**, shares what that journey looked like for her. Her story highlights the power of words and how they shape our beliefs.*

# DEDICATION

I dedicate this Chapter to the ones I hold dear, my husband Charlie, who is flying high with the angels. To my daughters and son-in-love, I pray you will always remember "Words are seeds, plant good ones." May the Lord always guide you in everything you do.

Cynthia Kelly

# DIVINE DIALOGUE
## HOW WORDS SHAPE OUR LIVES

## Cynthia Kelly

Entrepreneur, Business Owner

**Tennessee, USA**

*"In the stillness of the heart, the whispers*
*of faith become the loudest truths."*
~ Cynthia Kelly

### The Power of Intentional Words

I was sitting on the beach, toes buried in the warm sand. The sun shone brightly, casting a golden glow over everything, and the ocean breeze was perfect—gentle, refreshing, carrying the scent of saltwater and freedom. Yet my heart was heavy, weighed down by memories and unanswered questions. I was still in shock, trying to decipher exactly what happened on my graduation night.

The private Catholic school I attended was small, intimate. We had only about 68 students in our graduating class. We were a close-knit group, bound by shared experiences of school uniforms, the daily chapel before school for those who wanted to attend, glee club, drama club, sports and snowball dances. We all knew or knew of each other. When one of us was up to something, everyone would eventually know. Graduation night was supposed to be a celebration, a final gathering before we all went our separate ways. We were all together at a classmate's house for the party. It was a joyful evening, filled with laughter, reminiscing, and the excitement of the future.

Then everything changed in the blink of an eye. One of my classmates, Sharon, and a former graduate, were in a motorcycle accident. They were both killed instantly. The news was devastating, a gut-wrenching blow that shattered the night's festivities. The grief that enveloped our small school community was profound, and the sorrow lingered long after the initial shock had worn off.

What haunted me most, though, was something Sharon had said in class a month or so before that tragic night. Sister Louise, our Current Events teacher, had been asking us what we wanted to do after high school, a typical question for seniors. When it was Sharon's turn, she proclaimed, with an unsettling calmness and a giggle in her voice, that all she wanted was to graduate and die. It seemed like a morbid joke at the time, but now, with the eerie finality of her words, I couldn't shake the feeling that somehow, someway, her declaration had become reality.

My head and my heart were both reeling. She got what she said she wanted. *How could that be? Did one thing have to do with the other? Was it just a cruel coincidence, or was there something more to it?* These questions tormented me, and I found myself constantly replaying her words and the events of that night in my mind.

In the aftermath, I began to ask myself a lot of questions. Could I change the outcome of what I was going through or make the things I was reaching for come to pass by speaking them into existence? We all say random things, and we all think the wrong things. I do it daily, but Sharon's words and their apparent fulfillment started me on a journey of self-reflection and exploration about what I think, believe about the power of the words I use when facing situations I want to change.

A few years after this incident, I was sitting on my bed in the basement of my parents' house, devastated and feeling hopeless after my first husband abandoned me. In my despair, I found a book by Sandy Brown titled, *Is There Anybody Out There Who Can Help Me?* As I read the book, I came to a chapter where the author was in the bathtub getting ready to baptize herself. The book says her eyes fell on a scripture that talked about the gift of tongues. She thought if it was a gift, she wanted it too. Inspired, I thought I wanted it as well.

So, I stopped reading the book and, while sitting there on the bed, asked Jesus to save me. I also asked for the gift of tongues. I thought I would just do what she did, but I couldn't use "Yaba Daba Do" to start because she had used it (a silly thought, I know). So, I closed my eyes and just opened my mouth to start speaking. I must have prayed for at least an hour, speaking words I did not know. But this I can tell you with every emotion I did not have my own words for was coming out, and I could physically feel it lifting off me. I will never forget what the Lord did for me that night and the transformation in my heart and mind.

My peace was instantaneous, while the transformation of how I thought and believed was not. It was a gradual process of discovering a new perspective, a new way of understanding the world and my place in it. Through this journey, I found a method that I began to use to change the outcome of almost any situation.

I learned the power of belief. I frequently found that my initial thoughts about a situation were often wrong, skewed by fear, doubt, or negativity. But then, through prayer and reflection, God would show me the truth. Have you ever been there? I remember teaching my first sewing class. It was in my early 20s, a time when dreaming and talking about possibilities was easy, but taking action was daunting. The day arrived, and the classroom was packed with eager students.

The weight of the moment hit me, and I nearly backed out. Overwhelmed with fear, I locked myself in the bathroom, pleading with God, convinced I couldn't go through with it. I argued, listing every reason why this was destined to fail and how unprepared I felt.

In that moment of desperation, I struck a deal with God: I would stand before the class, but He would have to guide me. Trembling yet determined, I chose to obey and face my fears. To my amazement, the class went better than I could have ever imagined. Not only did I successfully teach, but most of the students even signed up for another class.

It's a humbling experience, realizing that your first instinct was completely off the mark and that there's a greater truth waiting to be revealed.

God's word says, *"For as he thinketh in his heart, so is he..."* (Proverbs 23:7). Belief is everything. These words became a cornerstone of my new understanding. They reminded me my thoughts were powerful, and they shaped my reality in ways I hadn't fully appreciated before. The Bible became my guide, a source of wisdom and insight that helped me navigate the complexities of life. This deepened my faith, teaching me that trusting in God's word and embracing positive, faith-filled thoughts could transform my experiences and lead to outcomes far beyond my expectations.

I also discovered that to change my beliefs, I had to change the words I spoke. The first chapter of the Book of John verses 1-5 tells us, *"In the beginning was the Word, and the Word was with God, and the Word was God. The same was in the beginning with God. All things were made by him; and without him was not anything made that was made. In him was life; and the life was the light of men. And the light shineth in darkness; and the darkness comprehended it not."*

These verses spoke to me deeply. They reminded me that words are not just sounds or symbols; they are powerful, creative forces that shape our reality. The words we speak are seeds that will produce a harvest. What harvest do you want to have? This was a profound realization for me. It meant that my words directed my thoughts and were not just fleeting ideas but had the potential to create and transform. As I delved deeper into God's word, I began to apply these principles to my life. I started to monitor my thoughts more closely, to be more intentional with my words. When faced with challenges, I turned to prayer and scripture for guidance, seeking God's truth instead of relying solely on my understanding.

One particularly challenging situation occurred a few years after I had begun this journey of faith. I was facing a major career decision, one that would significantly impact my future. Should I stay in Tulsa where I was living at the time and sell Real Estate or move back to Tennessee and Manage two Sewing Machine Stores? The uncertainty was overwhelming, and my initial thoughts were filled with doubt and fear. *What if I made the wrong choices? What if I failed?* These questions plagued me, threatening to paralyze me with indecision.

But then, I remembered the lessons I had learned. I took a step back, prayed for guidance, and reflected on God's promises. I turned to the Bible, seeking reassurance and wisdom. One verse that stood out to me was Jeremiah 29:11 (ESV), *"For I know the plans I have for you, declares the Lord, plans for welfare and not for evil, to give you a future and a hope."*

This verse gave me the confidence I needed. I realized that God had a plan for me, a plan that was good and filled with hope. I just needed to trust in Him and follow His peace. With this renewed perspective, I made my decision, and it turned out to be one of the best choices I've ever made. It led to new opportunities and growth that I hadn't even imagined.

Through experiences like this, I became more convinced of the power of belief and the importance of aligning my thoughts and words with God's truth. It wasn't always easy, and there were times when I struggled to maintain a positive outlook. But each time I faced a challenge, I returned to the principles I had learned, seeking God's guidance and trusting in His plan.

One of the most significant lessons I learned was the importance of speaking life into my situations. Proverbs 18:21 (ESV) says, *"Death and life are in the power of the tongue, and those who love it will eat its fruits."* This verse underscores the importance of my words. They could either bring life or death, positivity or negativity, hope or despair.

I began to speak life into every situation I faced. When I felt overwhelmed, I reminded myself of God's promises. When I faced obstacles, I declared that I could overcome them with God's help. When I encountered setbacks, I spoke words of hope and perseverance. This practice transformed my outlook and helped me navigate life's challenges with greater resilience and faith.

Looking back, I realize how far I've come since that fateful graduation night. The tragedy of losing Sharon was a catalyst for profound change in my life. It led me to question, to seek, and ultimately to find a deeper understanding of the power of thoughts and words. It brought me to faith, to a relationship with Jesus, and to a new way of living.

## Peace Along the Shore

Now, sitting on the beach with the sun shining and the ocean breeze caressing my face, I felt a sense of peace. The heaviness in my heart had lifted, replaced by a deep gratitude for the journey I had undertaken. I knew that life would continue to present challenges and uncertainties, but I also knew that I had the tools to face them.

God's word had become a light in my darkness, guiding me through the uncertainties and fears. It has shown me that belief is everything; as a man thinks, so is he. It had taught me that in the beginning was the Word, and the Word was with God, and the Word was God. These truths had transformed my life, giving me hope and a new sense of purpose.

As I stood up and brushed the sand from my feet, I felt a renewed sense of determination. I knew that the journey was far from over, that there were still many lessons to learn and challenges to face. But I also knew that I was not alone. With God's guidance and the power of His word, I could face whatever lay ahead with confidence and faith.

## Faith in Motion: Take the Next Step

My journey has taken me from a place of despair and uncertainty to one of faith and empowerment. Through the power of applying God's word correctly and faith in God, I've learned to transform my thoughts, speak life into my situations, and trust in God's plan. This journey has taught me the importance of belief and the profound impact of aligning my words with truth.

Are you aware of the power your words hold in shaping your reality? How can you begin to speak life into your challenges and trust in God's plan for your future?

Join me on a journey where we align your beliefs with God's promises and embrace the strength of intentional, faith-driven words. My coaching services are designed to guide you in speaking life into your challenges, deepening your faith, and unlocking a future filled with hope and purpose. Take the first step towards spiritual and personal transformation today—contact me to discover how my faith-based coaching can help you achieve a brighter, more empowered future. Let's walk this path of faith together!

"When we speak with intention, we invite miracles
into the ordinary moments of life."
~ Cynthia Kelly

# Cynthia Kelly

On the next page, you'll find a poem I wrote called,
"Whispers of Faith." My hope is that it encourages you
wherever you are today.

## Whispers of Faith

In the golden glow of a setting sun,
Where ocean breezes softly run,
A heart once heavy finds its peace,
In whispered truths that never cease.

Amid the grief of loss and pain,
In darkest nights, in pouring rain,
A light shines forth, a guiding ray,
Leading the soul to a brighter day.

With every thought, with every word,
A silent prayer, a hope deferred,
Yet in the quiet, God's voice is clear,
Transforming doubt, dispelling fear.

For as we think, so we become,
In faith and hope, we overcome.
The Word, our anchor, ever true,
In every storm, it sees us through.

So speak with love, and live with grace,
In every trial, seek God's face.
For in the silence, hearts will find,
The strength to leave the past behind.

# ABOUT THE AUTHOR

Cynthia Kelly is an entrepreneur, business owner, and certified life mentoring coach. Her passion lies in empowering women from all walks of life to embrace change and reach their full potential. Cynthia combines her extensive knowledge with a compassionate, faith-based approach, guiding her clients through transformative journeys as they strive to become better humans together. Her coaching style weaves together practical strategies and spiritual principles, offering a holistic path to personal and professional growth.

When she's not working, Cynthia finds joy in the simple pleasures of life on the farm. She delights in the rhythmic hum of her sewing machine as she creates unique works of art, enjoys peaceful walks with her three dogs, or savors the moments spent on the back porch making cherished memories with her family. As a lifelong learner, Cynthia is always eager to explore new things, whether it's a new hobby or a fresh perspective.

Faith is her anchor, and she finds great pleasure in a good Bible study and listening to her favorite preachers on YouTube. These practices enrich her spirit and keep her grounded, infusing her coaching with depth and authenticity. Cynthia invites those ready to embark on a journey of transformation to connect with her via email. Together, she believes they can turn dreams into reality.

**Find Me:**

Facebook: www.facebook.com/thesewingcenter.net

Email: info@womenrockinlife.com

# COURAGEOUS VOICES UNLOCKED

*There was a time when I would question everything, myself, God and others. But through my story, God has given me an unshakable confidence I never thought possible. The final co-author, **Catherine** shares her own transformation from shy and unsure to bold and confident in the gifts and the calling God has given her. She also shares how her healing was guided by support from her coach and a list of tips that can help anyone feeling a little unsure about their purpose.*

# DEDICATION

To my beautiful, loving gracious mother, Judith Nellie Eaton.

Your unwavering love, support, and belief in me have been my greatest blessings. I am eternally grateful to have had you as both my mother and my best friend. The privilege of your presence in my life is something I will forever cherish.

I eagerly await the day we are reunited.

With all my love,
Your daughter, Catherine

# HARMONY AND GROWTH
## THE JOY OF BOUNDARIES

## Catherine Anne Bolton

Qualified Primary School Teacher,
Home Tutor and Musician

**Shoalhaven NSW, Australia**


*"I can do all things through Christ who strengthens me"* (Philippians 4:13 NKJV).

## Early Challenges

Having lived with a very dominant father who was often angry and shouted a lot and was extremely hard to appease most of the time, my life was not easy or particularly happy in the home. I was often afraid of him and certainly was not encouraged to express myself in any way, shape or form. He had to be the boss. It was the era where children were seen—not heard. The man was the head of the house and that was that. I was not encouraged to stand up for myself at all. It didn't seem fair to me. At times I felt frustrated, especially when I did have something I wanted to talk about.

On the other hand, my mother was a very gentle, kind, and thoughtful person. Always juggling her husband's needs with the needs of the rest of the family, and often putting everyone else first. I believe she was anxious and tired, especially with three children to run after, but put on a brave front to everyone. Often, she would retreat and keep many of her own thoughts, needs or wishes to herself. She struggled to assert herself and as a result, I didn't learn those skills either. I learned to suppress my own thoughts, needs and wants in just the same way.

## Life on the Farm

I was raised on a dairy farm on the south coast, near Milton. Dad was a good farmer. He worked hard and provided well for the family. Dad's father and mother lived in the house across from us, which was great. I used to love being up there. Lots of gardening and cooking as well as house jobs. Nana was so patient, but Pop liked peace and quiet. So I would go home while he had lunch and a rest. I am sure that I talked a lot!

Everyone worked hard and we all had to pitch in. My two brothers and I had to help as well. Some jobs were not so much fun, like hosing out the dairy and bringing in the cows or laying down the irrigation pipes and sprinklers. If I didn't need to help on the farm, I would be in the house with mum. Mum was a great cook. Being a Home Science Teacher, I am sure I helped her. It wasn't until later, when we got to high school that she went to work.

I enjoyed going to school. The local school was small in those days with very dedicated teachers. There was lots of poetry, drama and music. I loved to sing in the choir. It was then that I decided that I wanted to learn and become a primary school teacher just like them. I decided when I was 12 years old, that was what I would be when I grew up.

During school, I was bullied by other children because of my eye problems and poor sporting skills… I would often cry and retreat from them… Thankfully, my friends were kind. A few of them had their own issues. They were kind to me. We kept together. Unfortunately, I never really learned how to stand up for myself, even now it's a struggle.

## Overcoming Setbacks

After finishing school in 1978, I went to Goulburn Teachers College and achieved my Diploma of Teaching Certificate. It was a challenge to get through my course, especially the classroom teaching aspect. I was very shy back then and definitely lacking in confidence which held me back. I loved the children. I had all the theories locked in but found classroom control difficult. I ended up failing my final practice teaching block due to sickness. I felt discouraged and defeated so I took a break for a year. During which I visited my old Kindy teacher. She took me under her wing and helped me. I volunteered at the school doing group reading and math.

Sometimes, I would teach lessons for different teachers as well as taking three School Religious Education classes each week. Later that year I went back and completed my final practice teaching and graduated in 1982. Finally, I had arrived and was a fully qualified teacher. I had struggled through many insecurities as well as challenges. At times I felt that I would not be able to complete this final step. I was physically and mentally drained.

In August 1982, I married my husband, who was a Science Teacher at Ulladulla High. We bought a property near Milton, called Wirrabara. This is where we built our home and started our own family. So, there was no time to teach as all my energy was taken up looking after the house and family. At this stage, I had 2 children, and they kept us on our toes most days. They were busy but fun days. Not much time for me.

We attended the local Uniting Church in Milton where many of our friends and family attended. My husband would play the organ, and I would help in the Sunday School. Church has always been a part of our lives. We were willing to help in any way possible, even learning the guitar.

My husband and I had many good years on our first property near Flat-rock, especially the first few years. Life was quiet and calm. We loved being out in the bush and close to nature. Sometimes I would spin up some wool and make Bennie's to sell in the local craft shop. I found this very relaxing. Occasionally, I would knit jumpers for my children. Patchwork was another thing I loved to do when I had some free time.

As time went on, my husband's parents and Auntie would visit us. They often stayed most of the day. There was not much privacy for us. It was hard even though they did help with the garden and on the property. We had beautiful vegetables and fruit trees which helped us out.

Unfortunately, I found it hard when they were there. Once they moved out of the city, they wanted to be with us most of the time. I was not able to deal with it well and eventually, it impacted my physical and mental health causing a lot of stress on our marriage and family.

I did find my husband's mother to be very challenging and domineering as she liked things to be her way—just like dad. She tended to take over and voice her opinions often, especially on the way I kept my house and raised our children. Her way was the best and she was very determined to let me know. I felt that my thoughts, feelings, and opinions were not good enough for her. I did try to challenge her on a number of occasions but to no avail. Once again, I could not stand up for myself, so in the end, I just went along with it.

## Struggles and Challenges

Our finances were very tight at this stage, which presented its own challenges. We did manage to pay the property off and move to a larger property closer to town. We called it Sunny Hill. During this time, my husband decided to give up teaching as he was exhausted, which left us with very little money to live and raise four children under the age of 5. This was a challenge. We became very frugal, doing the best we could. Even though we tried to make ends meet, it was not working well and we needed to make a change for the better.

In 1989, we sold our property down near Milton and moved to Nowra. We bought a dairy farm called The Pines in Jennings Lane. My husband's parents moved into the other house on the same property which was the year of much rain, so dairying was hard work, and we had much to learn. My father was very helpful, both financially and physically. Without him, it would not have been possible.

The following year Dad and Mum sold their farm in Milton and moved up to a nearby dairy farm. It was good having them close by. Our family was growing up. After a few years of being in Nowra, I was able to get work in some of the local schools. I did enjoy those days. I mainly worked in the smaller schools but only on a casual basis. It helped my confidence and gave me a good outlet away from the farm.

At this stage, we were attending the Nowra Uniting Church. Again, my husband was playing the organ most Sundays while I helped in Sunday School. We made some good friends during this time. There were a lot of young families and activities to be involved in.

## Finding Me

Also, during this time, we decided to go to Berry Uniting Church with some of our closest friends at the time. There were lots of young families. The church was very good. We loved it up there. Making friends was easy. Once again, my husband was playing the organ and I was involved in the kids program as well as joining the worship team as a singer and a choir member. I was really nervous, but it was what I wanted to do. My confidence grew as a result. I knew then that music is so important. I really loved those times.

We sold up the dairy farm in 2003 and decided to buy a property near West Wyalong and later at Condobolin. My husband is mostly out there farming, while I stay here in Bomaderry. All the children have grown up now and are off doing their own things.

Now there was some time for me to pursue some hobbies like reading and scrapbooking. I loved to take photos, especially of the family. I found some friends close by who shared a common interest. They helped me so much. There were many sessions of laughter and chatter. I really enjoyed those days. The photo albums were a great source of achievement. Later I made several photo albums for our church in Bomaderry and for the Nowra Town Band.

It was at this stage that we decided to change churches from Berry and attend Bomaderry Uniting Church. It was a small church then with only a few older members. It was in Bomaderry and very close by. It was convenient and we already knew a few people there. We were the only young family then, but that was fine with us. We trusted that God would bless us. We felt safe, accepted and loved. Not long after a few other families joined the church as a result we started the Sunday School up. I was teaching Sunday School and my husband was playing the organ when he was available.

The church was growing and changing. More young families joined, which was so good. I joined the church council and also started to play my cornet or trumpet at most services. My confidence was improving. I was very nervous, but it has always been a passion. I did learn the piano for two years. I could read some music, but it was a steep learning curve all the same.

I have always wanted to learn and to grow my own faith. Studying the Bible is another passion I have. I joined a Bible

Study group called Bible Study Fellowship in which I helped run the children's program. It was fun. Working with the children and helping them learn about God is definitely one of my passions. This helped my confidence.

Teaching is my main passion. So, I decided after this to resume teaching at Special Religious Education. I have taught at Terara Public School, Bomaderry Public School, Nowra Infants School as well as Greenwell Point Public School. To be able to share my love of God with the children was such a blessing. I wasn't very confident to begin with, but I trusted God to help me. He definitely has.

With my husband being away often, I've had time to pursue some other types of work. Over the years I have developed a passion to help children with learning difficulties. I decided to start home tutoring. Having a house in Bomaderry with a separate office space made this ideal. I only had a few students, but it was enough. It was so rewarding helping them grow and become more capable with their schoolwork. Mostly the children needed help in the area of math and language. I felt more relaxed this way. I did some extra study to improve my confidence and skill set.

Another passion I have is working with young children with mental and physical disabilities. My friend approached me back in 2012 and asked if I would like to work assisting children to and from the Havenlee Special School Program in North Nowra. It would be through the Department of Education. I was not sure at the time, but I was willing to give it a go.

I had never written a resume before, so my friend helped me. I got the job straight away. This was a new area for me. I was shy and scared. I didn't know how I would go. I was not so familiar with other types of physical or mental disabilities.

Up to this point, I had only ever worked with mild learning disabilities, not like these children. I had to complete many online courses to help care for these children. I have really grown to love this work. The children are so beautiful and special. At times I can even share my faith and love with them. I still use my teaching skills when I can. My caring and compassionate nature has certainly made my job easier. It can be challenging but really rewarding. My confidence has grown over time, especially with the extra training.

I was asked to run a Music for Fun Group for preschool children. This one was a paid job. Of course, I said yes. Teaching and music together is fantastic! It was a great opportunity. It was a team teaching situation for a few hours a week. So many great ways to enjoy music for all the young children.

I have always had a passion for music. I learned the piano and guitar when I was young. I became involved in the Nowra Town Band after our son wanted to learn a cornet. He found the cornet a bit hard, so switched to playing the Tuba. He was great at it. One day while sitting in on my son's lessons, the teacher encouraged me to have a go myself as he remembered that my grandfather used to play cornet years ago. So, that's how I started, and I have been doing it ever since. I was very nervous and shy, but I am much better now. Music brings so much joy to play and share with others. Two of my daughters have also been in the band as well. One is now a fully qualified music teacher. The love for music runs in my family which is great.

My involvement in The Nowra Town Band has been great. Not just as a cornet player but as an active committee member. The music is very challenging at times. Learning to read music better is so rewarding. There is even a junior band now. So, anyone can join and learn to play. Learning to play in a larger group is good as we learn to work with each other. I know that I have improved so much and so has my confidence. We perform at public functions as well as concerts. It's very different to playing at church. Both are good in their own ways, allowing me to step outside my comfort zone.

I have also joined another local choir in the past year called the Food of Love Choir. I am enjoying my time with them. Reading the music and learning different parts and harmonies is a real blessing. The choir performs in the local community. It is good to be a part of this group. I have grown in my confidence and my ability to sing.

## Peace and Purpose

A few years ago, I felt tired and overwhelmed with life verging on depression and frustration. It's been a long journey for me. My lack of confidence and being a people pleaser as well as my inability to say no to things and people had become a big problem. I found it hard to set boundaries and it was wearing me out. Fear of failure, lack of self-respect and confidence was not helping at all. Coupled with the fact that I found it hard to express myself, made life hard. Nothing seemed to help. I have tried counseling several times. It worked for a short while, but then things would start to overwhelm me again.

A trusted friend and coach has looked at my past with me, which was hard but well worth it. It's good to have a caring person talk and pray with you. She has helped me to face the things that I have hidden away for a very long time. We have talked and prayed over many issues. It is so important to confide in someone who's a good listener and prayer partner.

She helped me unlock past traumas and work through them. Being of a quieter and more sensitive nature, I often keep things inside. I have never been good at expressing or standing up for myself. I have now been given keys that I have been able to use. With God's help I will continue to grow in confidence and assertiveness in all areas of life.

These keys have really helped me grow in confidence and courage. I am now learning to set my own boundaries. Looking after myself and standing up for myself is imperative. By saying no to things, I leave room for the things that I want for me in my life. It's hard and it will be a life of continuous improvement, but this will allow me to pursue my passions in a much more directed way.

Here are some keys that have helped me to set boundaries.

1.  I have learned that it is ok to say no and that I don't have to give a reason.
2.  It's ok to say how I feel or what I think as I have a right to be heard.
3.  Be true to yourself. Taking care of your own well-being both physically and mentally.
4.  I have worthwhile opinions and ideas. My thoughts, ideas and feelings do matter, and I have the right to express these.
5.  To say what I need to say in a positive and confident way is ok.
6.  To believe in myself as I am a worthwhile person is what I need to do. I am capable of achieving many things. I am strong and can do what needs to be done.
7.  To be honest with myself. Be in touch with the things that matter to me and follow them and not allow other people or things to distract me. It's ok to be different.
8.  Believe in myself and my abilities.
9.  It's ok to care for myself. It's not selfish but necessary. Self-preservation is good.
10. By saying no to things, I will become less of a people pleaser and more of a God pleaser.

11. It's ok to own my thoughts and feelings. I can express them when needed,
12. To know that my talents and abilities are important and can be used by God.
13. To know that God is there for me and will help me through. To trust him and not worry so much.
14. Learning to trust God and leave all my cares with him because he loves me and wants the best for me always.

I have found having support and guidance has helped me so much. I am now a stronger person, and my confidence has improved. I am more at peace with myself, and I can express myself when needed. I now set boundaries and feel better about myself. As a result, I have more energy and direction in life.

As I reflect on my life, I can see a huge change over the years. I was very shy as a child. There were many situations where I was not confident. Having a mild disability as well as being very sensitive certainly has come with its own set of challenges. It has been a lifelong struggle, but I know that I have become more confident and self-assured.

Walking with God has been an amazing Journey. He has helped me through many of life's challenges. My shyness, insecurities and lack of confidence. Knowing that He is there for me has brought much comfort, strength and peace.

Step by step I have grown in my ability to trust God to lead, guide and protect. It has been a gradual process but well worth it. Through all this God has made me who I am today. I know that I am loved and have become a beautiful woman who is capable of many things. I am now able to use the gifts that God has given me. God has given me a passion for children, teaching and music of which I will continue to use with God by my side.

I am a gentle, compassionate person driven by a desire to help other people. I love my scrapbooking, sewing and reading as well as music. These are a blessing to me as well as others.

I have a desire to be an encouragement to other people who are in need. My ability to listen and show empathy helps in these situations. I believe that God has been there for me and has helped me overcome my disability and my challenging home life to a point where I am able to use my gifts to help others and bless them through my music and my teaching.

We all have our own challenges in life. It's how things are. We all need some help along the way to overcome and unleash our gifts and potential. It is the greatest blessing and will bring true peace and happiness. With this comes a growth in confidence as we go through life with a purpose which brings us closer to God.

Don't be afraid to chase your dreams. Unleash your potential. Become the person whom you were meant to be. This will bring you peace and happiness.

*Are you struggling with overcoming childhood hurts?*
*Are you struggling to let go of the past and move forward?*
*Are you living with a disability?*
*Are you feeling that life is too hard?*

May I encourage you to seek professional help through prayer counseling.

I have always known that God has been with me. When I was young, my grandmother would always sing as she went about her daily tasks or out in the garden. She was a beautiful example of a loving, caring woman of God setting a beautiful example for me.

I remember her singing "What a friend we have in Jesus" by William Rowlands (The Australian Hymn Book no 165) and Psalm 23 "The Lord's My Shepherd." Those words are so wonderful as they remind us that we can come to Him with all our needs and He will be there for me.

## Catherine Anne Bolton

Qualified Primary Teacher, Home Tutor and Musician

# ABOUT THE AUTHOR

Catherine Anne Bolton is a passionate and dedicated Primary School Teacher, home tutor, and accomplished musician. From the age of 12, she knew her calling was to be a teacher, driven by a deep desire to help others learn and achieve their life goals. As a mother of four grown children and a proud grandmother, Catherine is committed to supporting her family, nurturing their growth, and celebrating their successes.

Her extensive experience and qualifications in education have led her to various roles, particularly in supporting families and children with special needs through personalized home tutoring lessons. Catherine's love for music shines in her community involvement, where she plays an instrument, leads her church band, participates in a local town band, and sings with a choir.

With a love for travel and exploration, Catherine sees life as an exciting adventure and is always ready to discover new places. Her life is a harmonious blend of service to her family and community while ensuring her own needs are met and her life remains balanced and fulfilling.

**Find Me:**

Facebook: www.facebook.com/catherine.bolton908

Email: cbolton1960@gmail.com

Nowra Town Band:
www.facebook.com/profile.php?id=100032847713283

Contact the Nowra Town Band for training band lessons:
+61490830895

Facebook: Food of Love Choir.
www.facebook.com/FoodOfLoveChoir/

163

Facebook: Food of Love Choir.
www.facebook.com/FoodOfLoveChoir/

# COURAGEOUS VOICES UNLOCKED

As we bring Courageous Voices Unlocked to a close, we are overwhelmed with gratitude for the grace of God and His love for each of our unique stories. This journey has reminded us of our Heavenly Father's desire for us to live in community, embracing the beauty of our shared experiences. The stories in our book of courageous women sharing their voices have shown us the strength that comes from saying no, asserting our needs, and believing in our worth, all while trusting in God's plan.

As you turn the final page, we invite you to continue this journey of growth and self-discovery. Together, let's live authentically, free from the pressures of people-pleasing, and embrace the joy that comes from aligning with our true selves in God's love. If this has resonated with you, we extend a heartfelt invitation to join us in our next anthology focused on the transformative power of self-care. We would love to hear your story—your experiences, insights, and growth—as you've navigated the path of prioritizing your well-being.

Whether you're inspired to share your own story or eager to continue reading about the journeys of others, there's a place for you in our community. Your voice is valuable, and together, we can continue to uplift and inspire one another. Thank you for being part of this book.

We look forward to walking with you in the next chapter.

Carmel Austin & Stephanie Miller

For more information about our books and coaching services, don't hesitate to get in touch with Carmel at Carmel's Garden at www.carmelsgarden.com.